MW00908004

VOICE IN THE

DARK

Marissa Alexa McCool

Foreword by Dan Arel

Additional Essays by Melina Rayna Barratt,
Matthew O'Neil, Noah Lugeons, Karen Garst,
and Dr. Gleb Tsipursky

Voice in the Dark is a work of fiction. Names, characters, places, and incidents are either the product of the author's imagination or are used fictitiously. Any resemblance to actual persons, living or dead, is entirely coincidental.

Cover design by Terry Sheffield at Mind Aquarium
https://www.facebook.com/MindAquarium/

Published by Wyrmwood Publishing & Editing
http://www.wyrmwoodpublishing.com

ISBN-13: 978-1548184551
ISBN-10: 1548184551

ACKNOWLEDGMENTS

To my family, blood and chosen: without you, I wouldn't be who I am.

To my husband and partners: you make my heart beat the way it does.

To Amber, for dealing with my overwhelming desire to write and making it presentable. Support Wyrmwood Publishing!

To Terry, for knowing who I was at 19 and still being here. Also for your awesome artwork.

To the works *Pump up the Volume; Daria; Bang, Bang, You're Dead;* and *Empire Records*—thank you for reaching me in a way that none else have, and none have since.

To the Penn LGBT Center, for standing beside me as I became myself under your watch.

To Laura Jane Grace, for writing songs and melodies that speak to me, something I never experienced in music until I discovered *Against Me!*

To the *Silent Hill* soundtrack, for guiding nearly every word of this book as my background writing music. *Silent Hill: Downpour* more than any others.

To *The Scathing Atheist, Cognitive Dissonance, Opening Arguments, Gaytheist Manifesto,* and all the other podcasts who now consider me part of their community.

To those who spoke up for me, as I try to speak up for them.

To anyone who has bought any of my books, listened to my podcasts, read my blog, attended my events, or just reached out once—thank you. I wouldn't be able to do this if I didn't know it mattered to someone.

To Dan, Noah, Karen, Matthew, Melina, and Gleb—thank you for being willing to think highly enough of me to put your names alongside something I wrote.

To anyone I've ever upset with who I am, intentionally or not—I never meant to hurt you. I hope this story helps put that into a relatable context.

To you, if you're reading this.

To Aiden, Jeanne, Amy, Nathanial, Michael, Kieran, LaLa, Aaron, Monk, Eli, Anna, Tom, Cecil, Thomas, Andrew, Karen, Matthew, Callie, and Ari.

Thank you for helping me find my voice.

FOREWORD

Dan Arel

Doing the right thing sucks sometimes.

Yet when you believe what you are doing is right, it can make the loss of family and friends easier, in hindsight. At the time, it can be excruciating, and oftentimes leads many of us to instead do the wrong thing for what we think are the right reasons.

Growing up in a small town in New Hampshire, I was a skinny, dorky kid who was an easy target for bullies. I would get changed for physical education alone in a corner and would never dare take a shower after. I was the kid who would have their clothes stolen, be pushed over, or teased relentlessly for any bodily imperfection the bullies could find.

Even after I joined the ice hockey team in high school, I felt unwelcome and out of place with the other jocks who had been my bullies. I hated being in the locker room. I felt like an outcast. I felt unwelcome everywhere I went, and I felt unloved. Many of my friends had started dating and having sex, and I was going home to play NHL '95 on my PC.

I was lucky. I found something that made me feel special, heard, and a part of something. For me, it was music. I heard the angst of being different in hardcore music coming out of Boston. I found solace in the lyrics of Marilyn Manson and felt that I was welcome in these circles and far less judged. I could be myself, a freak in my own right, and I wouldn't be beat up, at least not by them.

Like I said, though, I was lucky. Yet every day, I read about kids who remind me of myself growing up. Kids who were not lucky. Music didn't reach them, or if it did, the problems they were dealing with far outweighed mine and it wasn't enough. Kids like the ones in Marissa Alexa McCool's *Voice in the Dark*. I found myself in these pages, hearing my story told, drawn to their own conclusions and left wondering if this could have been me if I hadn't been so lucky to find my outlet and voice.

Today, I don't even recognize the person I once was. The teenage me would have done what would have been least likely to get him beat up, but somewhere along the way, I became an adult who will do what is right, even if it ends up getting me beat up. While I have been fortunate in that arena, I have lost many friends over standing firm in my beliefs of what is right. Not standing aside as someone tells me that transgender men and women are not killed in the same way people of color were during the Civil Rights Movement, so I should never compare the two. Or being told that I should respect the personal rights of a man calling for the ethnic cleansing of America. People decided to end friendships with me over these stances.

It hurts to lose people close to me, but I must be a person of conviction and not convenience. I could have agreed with everyone above and still be their friend today, but who would I be when I looked in the mirror? Would having their friendship fill the void of knowing I was selling others short just so my life could be slightly easier? I am a straight, cis white male—I don't know if my life can get much easier, but it is certainly appealing to try. However, that wouldn't be the me I want to be. I could not live with that version of myself.

Voice in the Dark will force you to look at who you are and what kind of person you want to be. I read it while simultaneously challenging my own positions and asking if I could have done better for myself, but more importantly, the book made me ask questions that will never leave me: Could I have done more for someone else? Did I not stand up for someone when they needed someone the most? Did I allow someone else to be bullied so that the bully would pass me by? Can I live with myself if I let others destroy someone's life in an effort to not inconvenience myself?

The questions are uncomfortable, but necessary. They are what drive me, and likely you, to be a better person today than you were yesterday. It's what makes me a humanist. Marissa made me realize I can do better, even when I think I am doing my best. I can make sure that when I am making a decision based on a moral judgment, I am thinking beyond myself and ensuring that I am thinking of others.

As you turn each page of this book, allow yourself to see the world through the eyes of each character and realize there is a piece of you in all of them. Find each piece of who you want to be and who you don't. Put the book down determined to be a better person because of what you found that you liked and disliked in each. When you finish this book, I hope you do as I did and realize we can all do better, and decide once and for all that you're done making the easy choices in your life and from now on, you're going to make the right ones.

—Dan Arel, author of *The Secular Activist* and *Parenting Without God*

INTRODUCTION

Hard Harry spoke to me long before I knew how much it meant.

My formative years were in the late 90s, a time where counterculture was kinda cool, where *Daria* represented those of us who didn't buy into the pre-packaged crap that everyone else did, and where everyone knew when it was Rex Manning Day. There it was, a brief period of time—a few years where not going along with what everyone thought you should do was almost mainstream. We were represented, we had voices, and we felt a little bit more like our authentic selves.

Post-9/11 patriotism sort of ruined that, as anyone different was once again ostracized and accused of being un-American and divisive. Thankfully, that never lasted . . .

Here, in 2017, I finished this book . . . the fourth one I've published since coming out . . . while the president of our country is being accused of colluding with Russia to get elected. I wrote a book shortly after his election, which

I still feel to be one of the dumbest thing this country has ever done, and yes, that includes all the other bullshit too.

I never thought telling Trump to go fuck himself for 200-plus pages would ever lead people to knowing who I was. I didn't write it for that. I wrote it because so many years of not being who I was led to a powder keg of emotions that detonated when our country put a sexual-assaulting, Russian-colluding nimrod in charge of the nuclear arsenal and the free world. I no longer cared what anyone who supported this nutcase had to say, and I needed to speak up somehow.

Now, only a few months later, I'll be speaking at several more events all over the country. Overnight, a wealth of podcasts started inviting me as a guest, and they treated me like a voice that mattered. I was worried it was only the timing in which I'd finished the book of telling Trump to fuck off rather than the content, but even months later at ReasonCon in Hickory, North Carolina, people were still approaching the purple-corset-wearing Amazon with a purple Sharpie and buying copies of my book. It resonated with people, and those people stayed around even after knowing I was transgender. I couldn't fathom that happening even a year earlier.

When I told Pastor Carl, "I'm transgender, fuck you!" I didn't expect so many people from all over the world to reach out to me in the successive months. Speaking up had its good side—visibility, popularity, endless thank-you letters and admiration, guest spots, and bookings to speak to others.

But it came with its negatives too. Now I needed a

different last name, so as not to subject my kids to the danger that someone like Sophie LaBelle faced for, you know, existing. They didn't deserve that, and I did my best to shield them from it.

They didn't need to see the rape threats, the violent threats, those who encouraged others to harm us. They didn't need to see me cry as the weight of so much negativity caught up to me, despite my best efforts.

It comes with the territory of being loud, visible, and outspoken. I, as a transgender female in Trump's America, am a target for their bigotry, shitty opinions, and backward dick-slapping, overcompensating sense of fragile masculinity. I'd be lying if I said it didn't have its negative consequences, but I live with no regrets.

I'd much rather have spoken up and been mistaken than wondered what would've happened if I did. I could've stayed in the closet, pretending to be a married white male with kids, but that was a lie I could no longer tell, a mask I could no longer put on. I came out to the public only a short time ago, and recently graduated UPenn, class of 2017, with my true name and identity represented on my class ring, in the yearbook, and on my diploma. My husband has done the same. No regrets.

This book is a throwback to some of those movies and books I read when I was a kid. However, it's more about what it means to speak out, because a good portion of the world will urge you to let it go, calm down, and rejoin the status quo, happy and blissfully ignorant of the marginalized communities they'd rather not stick up for, lest it inconvenience their trip to Wal-Mart.

None of the writers who contributed to this book would say that speaking up and being vocal had no consequences either, and I hope you find their varied takes on the idea helpful and as inspiring as I find each one of them. I wouldn't be here without Noah Lugeons, especially, and his wife, Lucinda, my LaLa, who have been rocks, inspirational, and have shown me the utmost kindness and dignity at a time where I didn't know if I'd ever know what that meant again. They can downplay its importance as the way they would've treated anyone, and that's their right, but never mistake my love for them and how they brought me to where I am.

I love all of you, and these writers who have contributed to this book—I only hope to live up to their righteous indignation and bravery in the consequences, both positive and negative, of choosing to speak up rather than shut up. I hope you feel the same way after reading this as well.

Always take back your name. Never let them keep it. Stand up for those who are being bullied and marginalized, and never let anyone tell you that nothing will ever change. It won't be overnight, but it will happen. Do what's right, and be visible in the process. We need you, now more than ever. Thank you.

—Marissa Alexa McCool
May 27th, 2017

PROLOGUE

Columbus, 2009

COLUMBUS IS THE NAME OF MANY TOWNS AND CITIES.
This one is them. This one is all of them, and yet none
of them. It's no different from any other, and yet it is.
Does the name of the town really matter? It's generic,
like Main Street or numbers that start with 555: Once
you hear it, it stops mattering to you.

That's Columbus. That's this town. That's this year.
That's this school. Columbus Area High School: You
think nothing of it, and that's already more effort than
it deserves. Why would anyone care about Columbus,
or the kids who popped out of a womb there? Most of
the kids that do end up staying there, but not because
it's great. Because it's easy. Because it's convenient.
Because what the fuck else are they going to do?
College? Grad school? Army? What is there outside of
Columbus that you can't find there?

They always say it's the quiet ones you gotta watch.
Granted, I don't know who said that, or who "they" are,
but the quiet ones are usually contemplating. Figuring

1

out when they're going to speak and what they're going to say, and how to translate the mass of obscenities into something that can be consumed by another person; that's what goes on in the mind of those quiet introverts. Some of them. One of them. This story is about one of them. Or more. Your choice.

Another one of those clichés that isn't true is that bullies back down if you ignore them. People like to think that because it keeps them from the responsibility of action. It's much easier to do nothing than it is to do something. Doing nothing has no consequences, or so one would like to believe.

The truth is, bullies love unchecked power. Usually the first time they bully someone, they're expecting to get in trouble. When they don't, their confidence grows, and perhaps they gain allies. People of weak character and morals gravitate toward someone who makes other people feel bad. So coincidental.

It's much easier to talk about this weather. Do you think it's going to snow this year? I can't believe it's 75 in February. How about this wind? You don't risk anything by asking someone about the weather. It's like asking about the local sports team: even those who couldn't care less about it are going to fake it. Social contract. It invites someone in with no risk to either party, and is forgotten about just as quickly. The illusion of a connection was made, and then disappears without any of the responsibility that follows real exchanges of information. Bonds of friendship, don't those get tricky? Feelings get involved. Commitments. Who wants that? Better to just move on and go about your day.

Well, sometimes that monotony needs to be broken. Sometimes enough shit has gone down that the one voice out there, seemingly the only one who notices what is wrong, needs to speak up. To speak out. To call those out who are wrong, corrupt, sneaky, selfish, manipulative . . . dangerous.

Speaking up is not only good, but necessary. Without someone speaking up, power goes unchecked, corruption gets stronger, and observers see no resistance. But it doesn't come without its consequences, social and otherwise. Those in power want to shut up dissenters by any means necessary, and will often seek the means of doing so at the expense of the very people who are being exploited. The speaker becomes a target, an object of ire for those who would rather not have their day interrupted with the inconvenience of fact. Surely surviving and dealing with it is the better option. Staying quiet means you'll get left alone. It could always be worse. It could always get worse. Better not to be the one they come looking for.

This is a story about someone who made the harder decision. But don't take my word for it.

Take theirs.

VERONICA

MY HEAD FINALLY HIT ITS HAPPY PLACE: THE SOFT, fluffy pillow on my best friend—my bed. My poor head was overloaded with another week of bullshit from Columbus Area High School, home of the . . . I didn't know, and who cared? Eventually I'd be gone, and they'd forget all about me, as they should. I'd done nothing to deserve recognition.

I glanced at my phone. Shit! It was almost time!

My computer flickered to life, and rather slowly at that. This old desktop was going to be the death of me. I was pretty sure it still had Windows XP as its operating system. But it connected to the Internet, and that was what I needed at this moment. I needed the Internet. I needed the site. I needed . . . him.

It took a few seconds, but I heard the sound of a Skype connection. He was coming on, as he always did. His was the one voice I wanted to hear. He was the one willing to say the shit that nobody else would, the stuff that was in my head, but I knew I could never risk speaking out about. They'd find a way to get rid of me if

4

they did. That was what life here was. That was what the Columbus life was: protect the mass idea of people and kids, even if you have to go against the consent of every last one of them.

Except one. Except him. Speak to me, voice in the dark. Take me away for a little while. It's all I ask.

"Do you ever feel like you don't belong anywhere?" he asked rhetorically, but I nodded in agreement anyway. "Like you're constantly on the outside looking in?"

"All the time," I responded, even though I knew he couldn't hear me.

The lights flickered off downstairs. Good, my parents weren't going to bother me. It was just me and him, and whoever else was listening, but I couldn't imagine many of the numbskulls I went to school with paying attention to something like this. He made me think, and thinking's hard. It hurts the brainy parts.

"Through no fault of your own, do you seem to be looking through a glass wall, carefully kept away from those in charge and those considered desirable by the masses around you?" His voice. The voice. Yes, that was what I was thinking right now! He said it better than I could have. Mine would have had more "fucks" and "ums."

"I'm tired of it. I'm sick of having to put on a happy face so I don't come off as a threat to my fellow students," he ranted. Wasn't that the truth? Ever since the bomb threat last year, the school had gone overboard with their security policies.

This morning, there was that kid with the spiked hair. I think his name was Brian, but I wasn't sure. He never liked anyone, so I didn't bother to ask. But looking like that, as one would expect, draws attention to yourself, which was why I didn't do it. I would've loved to wear the t-shirts saying *Fuck Off* like he did, but I didn't have the courage or the gall.

He was sitting outside this morning, minding his own business, and the only crime? Existing in the space of someone in power. The nerve! The head security guard . . . pretty sure his name was Don . . . grabbed him by the jacket and pushed him toward the entrance.

"We don't want any trouble today, now do we?" he asked him in that condescending douchebag tone that authority figures always seem to have.

"Fuck off, you low-grade rent-a-cop!" Brian had argued back. So many of us wish we could say that to security. He was the only one who did so, and it made him a target for searches and detention. That was why none of the rest of us did it. Well, except for the Voice, but I didn't know who he was. For all I knew, nobody did.

"I'm sick of being told to cheer up, that I'll develop frown lines if I don't smile more, or that I'll miss out on so much if I don't join the crowd and have fun. These are the good times, the best times, right?"

"Yeah, right," I sarcastically remarked out loud.

His train of thought apparently lined up with mine yet again: "Every movie made tells me how great the 90s were, so why shouldn't we be living it up?"

Because movies are made to convince us that our lives suck and would be better if we ran away and stalked the person we found hot until they gave in and liked us back. Real world shit, you know?

6

"What is it that I'm missing? Keg parties? Or maybe raves. Maybe even better yet, I'm missing out on drinking from a keg while being at a rave while some of that good nostalgic music plays."

Holy shit, was 90s nostalgia overblown these days! It was eight years after 9/11 and we were still looking to the time before everyone had to be screened to go into their own school. Sure, it was only elementary school back then, but those were better times, right? They had to be. They couldn't be worse than this . . .

Could they?

"Every other article posted online tells me how if I remember some obscure reference to growing up, that my childhood was awesome, so clearly, that's how I should be feeling about my own. 'Hey, if you remember this Ninja Turtle toy, your childhood was awesome!'"

Yeah, toys. That's what made the difference. Not having Dad at home without him smelling like a bar floor. Not having Mom check my homework, or at least consider what I wanted for dinner—just the toys that they bought us to shut us up for a few seconds. Those were the keys to happiness.

But at least I had this. At least I had one friend I knew I could count on, even if he didn't know who I was. Or maybe he did, and I didn't know it. For however long he spoke to me, though, it didn't matter. In my room at night, it was me and him, and the rest of the world could fuck off.

Especially CAHS.

JESSE

I BANDAGED UP MY LEFT WRIST, BITING OFF THE END OF the tape with my teeth. My right hand slid the sleeve of my shirt back down over it completely, hiding it from sight. Who needed reminders?

"What is it I'm missing?" the voice asked on my computer. The sound shook me from my hypnotic state. I'd almost forgotten that I'd tuned into the website that I'd heard people talking about. The voice; the one willing to speak out about how fucked up this school is—was it true? Was there one really out there who saw what I did?

"Keg parties—yeah, that's it," he suggested. "Or raves. Those parties they always talk about on the news where people shoot vodka in their eye or something."

That's not exactly what raves are, but points for trying, dude. Raves were mostly made up of kids like us, people who were sick of being told who they were and had a place to do something about it. Almost no one spoke to each other because they got lost in the music, and there are few things more freeing than the ecstasy of a song.

"Maybe even better yet, I'm missing out on drinking from a keg while being at a rave while some of that good nostalgic music plays. Every other meme posted online tells me how if I remember some obscure reference to growing up that my childhood was awesome."

Childhood? Weren't we still children? Wasn't this the time we were supposed to be making nostalgic memories, not reliving them? Still, he had a point: 90s nostalgia was out of control, especially among people who barely lived in them.

"So clearly, that's how I should be feeling," the voice continued. "About my own, right? Hey, if you remember this Ninja Turtle toy, your childhood was awesome!'"

I stopped staring at the wall, standing up and walking across my room to the mirror. As I was sliding up my left sleeve again, I noticed the metal binding I used and remembered that it would never make it through security. Yeah, security, at a high school, and they made no secret of the fact that people like me were the targets.

They'd gotten Brian this morning. It was worse than the airport, at least as far as I could tell. Scanning with metal detectors, rifling through bags with latex gloves, they'd held up an old-school pipe that Brian had in his bag this morning. "Contraband!" the one officer called out, as if she'd found the Ark of the Covenant, finally justifying the money that had been poured into school security. Of course it was Brian. It was always going to be Brian.

Don, the head security guard, grabbed him by the jacket and escorted him away as he pleaded that it was a gift—like that mattered. Don gave no fucks about anyone but the pretty ones, and even that was questionable. Our mission was to contribute to school spirit and morale, or be the downfall of it.

I knew where I stood.

BRIAN

THAT PESKY SON OF A BITCH SECURITY GUARD NEARLY tore my jacket as he dragged me to the principal's office . . . again. I think he got his rocks off at night with the smell of my cologne. Why else would he touch me so much?

There was another poor kid who violated some measure of the Thought Police Acts of 2009, and he was a first-time offender, clearly. Guy didn't even realize how fucked the system truly is.

"What are we doing here?" I snapped at Don, hoping to at least get a wet spot in his wrinkled khakis out of it.

"We'll see what the principal has to say about your behavior," he said, repeating the oath that I'm sure helped him sleep at night. Principal Fuckface, telling me how I would never reach my potential if I didn't fit in and stop being a distraction. Interesting how my clothes were a distraction but the cheerleader skirts weren't. Coincidence? Not likely.

There was no way I was sticking around to be

yelled at like every other day. There were better things to do. I got up as soon as Dickhead Don was out of view and reached for the door handle.

"Aren't we supposed to wait to see the principal?" Cute kid, had to be a freshman, but damn if he didn't have a lot to learn.

"You wait," I replied apathetically, not even wanting an argument or to give an explanation. "I've got enough to do as it is without this."

"You might get suspended for this!" I heard him yell after me. Oh, no, not that! Days where I wouldn't be legally required to show up to be treated like the criminal of Columbus High! What torture. How would I ever forgive myself?

The door of the digital media lab creaked open, and someone stepped aside as I tried to get through, as if they might get a disease from touching me. No matter.

"I DON'T NEED VIDEO GAMES, AND I DON'T THINK I'M missing a whole lot by not playing them," the Voice said to me later that night, obviously altering his voice. How was he getting away with this? Had to be one of the preps going undercover, or something.

"People act like this is a key—a missing part, if you will—of society that renders you invalid if you aren't an active participant," he continued. "That you need to grow and accept whatever changes come because you'll be left behind if you don't. As if I have to play the most recent first-person shooter to be a valid member of society."

I glanced over at my entertainment center, increasingly covered in dust. I hadn't touched the NES in years, and honestly didn't know if it even still worked. Not that I had any intention of using it, anyway. Why piss off the old man further by looking like I enjoy something?

I lay back, holding my hands behind my head to ease the headache of annoyance. Tomorrow, Don would probably fuck with me again. Tomorrow, they'd find a reason to send me to the principal. Tomorrow, they'd find another way to single me out as the root of all their problems.

But at least for now, for this moment, someone seemed to be on my side, rather than automatically taking the latter. Even if I had no idea who this guy was—and I didn't—someone was speaking for me instead of to me.

That was a rarity at Columbus.

BRIAN

HIS GAIN WAS SLIGHTLY LOUD, SO I TUNED IT A LITTLE bit, only enough to save the speakers for those listening to it aloud, if there were any out there.

I didn't know who he was, and he took every precaution to keep his identity secret from even me, so I respected that by not trying to find out. He asked me to run the technical stuff for his anonymous podcast about the school, and my job was to do just that. Nothing else.

I didn't agree with everything he said. Hell, more often than not, I found him a bit brash. But I also believe in the rights of speech and dissent, and I knew that it wasn't easy for kids in Columbus these days who didn't fit the mold.

I was never going to have any trouble with the administration. If I couldn't play sports, I got them money and improved their overall GPA, so I was safe. It would've been irresponsible, however, to leave that as it was and not do something to help others. Unfairness is still unfairness, even when it's not happening to you.

VERONICA

PEOPLE ALWAYS GOT OUT OF WILL'S WAY WHEN HE walked down the hall. He thought it was because they were afraid of him, but I knew better. It was because nobody wanted to even get considered for the zero-tolerance policy by smacking him in the face for being a dick. And he was a dick, but I liked him anyway . . . for some reason. Did high school relationships really matter that much?

Heather, a junior girl dating one of his friends, lifted up her flip phone to take a picture of us. Why not? It'll end up on Facebook with everything else, as long as she looked perfect . . . which she always did.

Will shoved a young kid out of the way for the crime of standing on his locker, and I groaned. Nobody touched the guy, but he could do whatever he wanted. I was waiting for the day where he'd decide I wasn't worth his time, either. I'd be grateful for the free time in my schedule. For now, it would be social suicide to dare do anything to upset him. I had less than a year left, and I didn't want to spend it in exile.

Leaning up against the locker next to him, I slid closer, giving the illusion that I was much fonder of him than I actually was. "Are you going to St. Pete's tonight?" I asked, hoping he'd do something that made me happy at least once during my tenure.

"That's kid's shit, Veronica," he snidely remarked. He wasn't entirely wrong, but it was where a lot of us hung out, anyway. We were left alone there and the food was free; not the greatest hangout of all time, but better than anything else in this dumb town. For anyone under twenty-one, anyway.

"Just come, Will," I pleaded without any emotion behind it. "Everyone else is going."

He didn't answer me, and I soon saw why.

A young . . . boy, I think . . . wearing long sleeves on a hot day and eyeliner had the nerve to walk by in slim pants in Will's vicinity. Will, like the full-grown adult he obviously was, tripped the kid, who probably affected him with weakness by existing.

The kid sprawled at Will's feet, losing everything he had with him, and turned beet-red. Will laughed and high-fived the douchebags he hung out with, and for a brief second, I saw the bandages on the kid's wrist. Fuck, Will. Great going.

I gave the kid the most sympathetic face I possibly could, knowing how little that would actually help, but the effort mattered, maybe? Offering him a hand, I knelt down to try to help him up . . . still assuming it was a him and not an androgynous girl . . . but he kicked away, nearly catching my hand, and sped away. I didn't blame him. If I saw someone hanging out with Will, I'd probably avoid them too.

"Do you have to be an asshole all the time?" I asked Will, knowing full well the answer. The effort at least eased my conscience.

"Don't tell me you feel bad for that little fag," Will chided. I hated that word so much, but I couldn't be seen criticizing the prized football player. "He'll take off the chick makeup, or he'll keep hanging around with the other losers."

So he was a guy, or at least he was right now. These days, you never could make assumptions—unless you were an asshole, and Will was indeed an asshole. However, there was a small morsel of truth within what he said, even though I doubted he saw it that way. Having the guts to express yourself came with consequences, especially here. Social and class warfare were emboldened by the security policies and preferential treatment of students, and going against that grain was begging for trouble. It sucked, but what were you going to do? You can't change the system.

"How enlightened of you," I muttered, not intending it to be loud enough to hear, but he did.

"Hey!" he shouted. I should've turned around and walked away right there, but as my mother always said, I was being stupid and not listening to my instinct. His powerful hand gripped my wrist almost tight enough to break it and whipped me around back to face him. Such beautiful eyes he had. Why were they filled with such raw anger? What did he have to be mad about?

"Knock it off, Will." I helplessly resisted, trying to free my wrist.

"If you're gonna keep dating me," he warned, "you gotta knock this shit off."

I finally got my wrist free, and I rubbed it as feeling returned to my arm. What was the point of fighting? Once I got into college, I could get the hell out of this place and none of it would matter.

I saw them heading up to the cafeteria. Not wanting to be left behind, despite everything, I chased them down to catch up. God forbid you be an individual. Nobody wanted to be an individual in this place.

Except him, anyway.

JAMES

VERONICA CHASED DOWN WILL AND THE OTHER GIRLS he was fucking behind her back. I leaned against my locker, enjoying the show as I always did, with my gorgeous girlfriend standing beside me.

"Did you see him grab her wrist like that?" Heather asked, concerned for her friend.

"Let it go, Heather," I warned, not wanting to incite anything that would cause a fight. "You'll become a pariah if you try to start anything with Will." I knew from experience, as I'd seen it happen. Nobody stood up to him, because there *was* no standing up to him. I at least had my dad working at the school, but that didn't mean a thing next to the charisma and pull Will had around here.

We went into our next class, and that fucking nerd kid was trying to push past me. I was going to let it go, but I knew the image I needed to maintain, and I smacked the books out of his hand. "What's your hurry?" I teased, dying a little inside by torturing this kid, but that was what we had to do to stay alive.

"James, is that really necessary?" Heather asked, similar to Veronica earlier. They were both right, but I couldn't let *them* know that. Before I could think of a good line to snark back at her, someone else approached.

My eyes followed the boots up to the dark kid that sat in the back of the room. His black t-shirt gripped his body like he was an athlete, but I'd never seen him in any locker rooms, so it wasn't from sports. The guy handed the books back to Mark, and I felt terrible that he had to go through that. Better him than me, though.

"Thanks, Lucas," said the nerd to the guy who was allowed to be a real person. *Lucas,* I thought to myself, *I'd hate to be you alone later in the hallway.*

"No problem, Mark," the kid responded. I realized I'd never heard him speak in this class before. He was physically intimidating, even though he was nowhere close to being Will's size. Then again, who was at Columbus?

I gave my best bully laugh as I sat down. Couldn't let anyone in the class start getting ideas. God, this whole thing was stupid, but what can ya do?

The new teacher walked in the room, and hot damn, she couldn't have been much older than us! She was smoking-hot too. She wrote her name on the dry-erase board. *Miss Hunter,* I thought. *I'd like to do a little hunting of my own!*

"Class, my name is Miss Hunter," she said, "and I'll be filling in for the rest for Mr. Dean for the rest of the semester."

Hell yes!

"Now, I'm sure you've already heard this," she

began, and I tuned out. More security bullshit, and fortunately, it didn't pertain to me. Well, fortunate for me, not so much for others. "But I'm required by Columbus Area High School to say it. Security in this school is of the utmost importance, and all of the protocols listed in your handbook are to be followed." Her voice was dead; she clearly didn't want to say this any more than we wanted to hear it.

"That includes no sharp objects, no weapons or firearms, and nothing that could be used as one. No lighters, no cigarettes or other smoking materials, and no alcohol or anything promoting the use thereof."

Right, nothing fun, I thought.

"You are also not to wear any shirts with brand name logos, as to not make anyone else feel bad, and obviously nothing inappropriate, either. The only acceptable brand logo is that of CAHS. All others will be confiscated."

Logos, the true root of the problem. What a fucking crock. I groaned with the rest of the class, even though I knew as well as anyone that it wasn't her fault.

"Now, onto the semester, as we'll be spending a lot of time together over the next few months."

"She's pretty hot, huh, bro?" some dude next to me asked.

"Yeah, I could get used to this," I responded, trying to be subtle . . . and failing.

"There will be writing assignments in this class," she suddenly announced, "and none of them will be done with your smartphone. I'm not an idiot; nobody randomly looks up and down that frequently for no reason."

The stir in the room drew all our eyes to some kid trying to use his backpack to hide it. The power of shame, Miss Hunter. Well-played.

While I was distracted by watching others, Miss Hunter grabbed my own phone from my desk. The ire in my chest rose, and I couldn't restrain myself.

"Give it back, Blondie," I said, suddenly hating the sound of my own voice.

"I said that phones needed to go away," she chided. "Your notifications will have to wait until after class."

"I don't accept it."

How was this so easy for him? The Voice said all the things I wanted to, but had no way of doing.

"I'm not actively seeking their approval, and it's pretty sick that our value as people is defined by what things we participate in. Those things that are created to subdue us and keep us from thinking for ourselves."

"Or acting like it," I added, even though he obviously couldn't hear me.

"Get the shiny new computer, or you're obsolete. Get the newest phone, or you're a relic. Irrelevant. Holding onto the past. They're all distractions. Keep the majority happy, and the outliers will just fade away."

As much as I didn't want him to be right, he was. All I could do was not be an outlier.

LIZ

MY PARENTS FOUGHT AGAIN LAST NIGHT, AND ON TOP OF that, it happened while Sean was over. It would have been embarrassing, if it wasn't so agonizing to hear yet again. They were both determined to never get divorced, but all they did anymore was fight. There didn't seem to be any love left in their relationship.

The bell rang, and I spotted him where I always did—by the steps near the buses. I felt bad for him; he didn't need to be put through the wringer with me. Maybe it'd be better if I broke up with him now so he didn't have to deal with my screaming parents and my emo bullshit.

"Are you listening tonight?" I asked him, partially out of curiosity to see if he really listened to me, and partially because it had become an outlet for me. Where two voices were yelling at each other, one spoke to me through the darkness and seemed genuinely interested in actually solving a problem. Perish the thought.

"Haven't missed it since you turned me onto it!" he gleefully replied. That surprised me. I still didn't think he had even watched a full episode of the Nostalgia Critic, and I tried showing him that at least a year ago.

Sean slipped his hand into mine as we did our best to weave through the crowds. "Does anyone know who he is?"

"I guess he goes here, but outside of that, no. Nothing. Not that I've heard, anyway," I added, hoping he didn't think that I was aware, either. Last thing I needed was more focus on my own broken home life.

A shadow blocked out the sun behind us, and I realized the head of security was looming over our conversation. "I wouldn't be caught listening to him, kids," he cautioned, as if we were five. "There will be serious consequences for anyone promoting that material around here."

The guy stormed away like he was some sort of secret agent on a mission. Christ, it was school security, not Hopkins or something.

Sean broke the awkward silence. "Think anyone else has figured it out?"

"What?"

"I mean, what does he do?"

"I think he's trying to follow the zero-tolerance policy," I admitted, hoping that was the case.

"I mean the podcast, Lizzie," he chided. Dammit, my cheeks flushed red. I'd guessed wrong again, and he was calling me Lizzie like that blonde chick on the kid's show. He knew I hated that. Why did he keep doing it?

"He comes on live, never leaves a recording, and then disappears," Sean mused, mostly to himself, I assumed. I was done guessing the wrong thing and humiliating myself.

Sean didn't listen to me any more than my parents did. I had enough to deal with without wondering if he gave a damn about me, either.

THE VOICE

THE SCREEN LIT UP WITH THE ANNOYING SOUND EFFECTS of the Skype connection. All the time the Internet's been around, and I don't think it's changed once. It's become universal; they even use it in movies now.

I glanced to the wall, where my tattered *Empire Records* poster still hung, despite the damn cats tearing it down because they went after the pushpins constantly. *Damn the Man,* I thought to myself. I had to; it was essentially the only identity I had.

My copy of Carlin's *Last Words* leaned against the screen. He'd died a year ago, and even though I wasn't around for much of his career, it still shattered me. The man was a lyrical genius and he didn't even sing. It was the rhythm, the poetry, the precision of every word he threaded throughout a profanity-laced tirade that spoke to me.

With him gone, I started saying what was on my mind; first to myself, then into a computer microphone, then on some broadcast channel that nobody knew. Mark was running tech for me, but I'd contacted him anonymously as my online handle: NamelessStateofDenmark. Yeah, I was a bit obsessed with *Hamlet*, but good luck discussing that with the cretins I went to school with.

Reclining in my computer chair, I rested my head against the built-in support. Mark was working his magic, as he always did for me. Good thing he did too, because I didn't have a clue beyond saying the words and hoping I didn't get caught. I had no idea what kind of hacker shit he was pulling, but it worked. That's all that mattered right now.

People were listening. I knew they were; I heard them discussing it around school more and more. The temptation to come out and tell them that I was the Voice, that I was the one speaking out against this bullshit, was strong, but I knew I couldn't. Saying the shit that I did got Carlin arrested and televangelists condemning him at every turn. High school was annoying enough without bringing hellfire and brimstone into it, though I imagined they weren't much different, from an objectively comparative standpoint.

My eyes followed the messy book wall, realizing I needed to either get a new bookshelf . . . again . . . or reorganize so that there'd be more room.

"I can't be the only one who realizes that they're taking us for fools," I began mindlessly, "stripping us of our individuality under the guise of communal bliss."

I thought of the kids who were being sent home for dress code, or because the security guards wanted to be dicks. It didn't really matter. There wasn't anything you could say back to them. It got you in deeper, and who needed that kind of attention? All of us at this shithole of a place in a nothing town wanted to graduate and let the townies stay here and raise the next generation of misanthropes, while those of us who realized there was life beyond Columbus got the fuck out and never looked back.

"Enforcing dress codes so we don't dare think of each other as different, selling abstinence so we don't have any fun while we're young, and treating cigarettes, pot, booze, and sex as if they lead to forever being tarnished."

It was no secret how they treated the so-called "undesirables." The administration didn't call them that—they wouldn't get the reference.

"Why are we seeking their approval?" I rhetorically asked, as if anyone had the ability to respond on this closed network. Sometimes I was really fucking stupid, but asking questions with no answers seemed to be a good way to provoke a response. So why not go with it until I found something better, or at least found an answer?

"What do we care if we are acceptable in their eyes? Didn't they do this when they were younger? Didn't they experiment, get wild, have a little fun, break the rules every now and then?"

I couldn't speak for everyone, but I'd seen the pictures of my parents in those old albums gathering dust in the basement. They were flower children, no doubt about it, so I knew their concern over me possibly smoking pot was full of shit. They were dropping acid like it was going out of fucking style when they were my age.

"You're telling me they were obedient consumers who followed the trends and never lashed out, never bucked the new gadget?" My dad had a fucking Pet Rock, for Christ's sake!

I sighed before I continued. This was gonna be a long one. I wasn't aware if I had five listeners or five hundred, but it wasn't important. Someone out there was listening. Someone out there had a voice. Someone out there *needed* a voice.

Sometimes, we need to know we're not alone. If I could help one kid at this godforsaken place know that, at least I'd be contributing something before I pissed on the wall and tore up my meaningless diploma one day. Dad had my entire future planned out; he wanted me to be just like him.

It's so nice when people feel they have the right to make all your decisions for you!

MARK

THE VOICE WAS ON TONIGHT. I STILL HAD TO MEET MY raiding party, but I could multitask without much trouble.

I wasn't one of those people who were unable to focus on people talking if I was also playing a game or something. I pitied those who were—it was the only way I was able to stay up late getting work done while also managing to have some sort of life . . . an online one, anyway.

My doorknob turned, and I immediately pushed the power button on the speakers. Last thing I needed were questions from the old man. The Voice might say some swear words, and Mark can't hear any of that!

"What are you listening to?" he demanded, as if I were on suicide watch and somebody might drive me over the edge.

"Nothing, Dad," I groaned. "Just playing my game," I added, hoping that would make him go away quicker. If he hated anything more than movies above a G rating, it was PC games.

"I wish you'd quit that shit," he snarled. "it's a waste of time."

Right, Dad, check. God forbid I do something fun once in a while that doesn't involve your parochial taste.

The door closed, so at least he was gone for now. Clicking the power button back on, I fiddled with the mixer, as the sound waves were hitting red. He must've been on a rant tonight. Good for him—beat the hell out of the old man's "you damn kids" speech every night.

"They call us rebels, outsiders, non-conformists, as if that's supposed to immediately end all hope of finding our own identity," the Voice explained. "They don't want us to find our own; they want us to find *theirs*. They want us to be just like they think they used to be, so they don't have to worry about us finding our own way and leaving them behind."

Damn, Voice . . . a little close to home there.

I closed the game out. The raiding party would have to go on without me, at least for a bit. Turning off TeamSpeak despite a series of vocal protests, my elbows held me steady as I got closer to the screen. I knew this didn't mean anything since he, you know, couldn't see me . . . but I was paying extra close attention after that little bit. Maybe this wasn't only complaining about school. Maybe there really was something more to it that I hadn't heard yet.

VERONICA

WILL CAME WITH US TO ST. PETE'S, BUT I KNEW HE couldn't just come with me and have a good time. He had to remind me that he was doing me a favor by acknowledging that I was a person and not a Stepford Girlfriend, so every moment was served with a fresh helping of teenage guilt.

James and Heather were drinking together out of red Solo cups. God knew what was in there, but I wasn't really interested. Once Will started impressing people with his belching skills, I snuck in a headphone to one ear while I pretended to dance along with whatever terrible music they were playing this week. It was always terrible; the only thing about it that changed week after week was the degree of terrible that it was.

". . . if we wear the wrong clothes, or post the wrong thing on Facebook, or don't eat up the latest pop sensation that gives us a trend to follow . . ." the Voice yelled into my ear. I nearly had to pull it out to avoid ear damage. Must've missed something tonight; it took him longer than this to get this riled up most of the time.

"What exactly is my life missing if I'm not expressing everything with a sideways winky smile? Is my life forever improved because I was able to turn punctuation into a shitty form of communication rather than being a fucking person?"

"It's overrated," I told myself out loud, watching Heather and James start to make out. Like I didn't already feel nauseous from the body odor and sweat surrounding me. What the hell was I doing here?

Seriously, what was I doing here? I was with a guy I hated, even though I let him fuck me once in a while. Our double date partners were so drunk that they might start banging on the dance floor before the Catholic overlords at this place noticed. I hated the music, and I hated our school and nearly everyone in it. This wasn't me.

I turned to a dirty mirror that looked like it belonged in a gas station bathroom. I felt ashamed, even as the smudge blocked out my face. *Good,* I thought. *It's better that way.*

MISS HUNTER

THE FIRST DAY COULD'VE GONE BETTER, BUT I'D HAD much worse when I was student-teaching—or even worse, subbing. I might as well have painted a target on my ass with those teenage boys when that happened. Showing a movie always seemed to work, but there was no real enforcement. It wasn't like the principals of those schools were ever going to back me up. I was the hippie, the nerdy librarian; the principals I knew had voted for McCain, and they stared at me like I'd helped Osama bin Laden himself.

And my mother had the nerve to ask if I had any prospects. Oh, yeah, I'm overrun with opportunities in this town.

Shit, I'd forgotten to find that link. The security guy, Don, had told me about some anonymous student verbally thrashing the place, and that sounded conducive to my mood at the moment. Probably some kid bitching that they don't have soda machines in the cafeteria, but it couldn't hurt to give it a try.

Once I had the page up, I shuffled the papers on my

desk as I tried to make sense of Mr. Dean's notes. How was I to translate any of these chicken scratches? Christ, were they reading *The Call of the Wild*? To a senior-level AP class?

"Tell them no," a modified voice said, derailing my train of thought.

"I'd sure like to," I answered out loud, even though that was pointless.

"Tell them that's not what happened. We know it's been sanitized. We know America wasn't always the white knight, running in to save the day. We passively accept this bullshit. They're teaching us not only what they want us to think, but how to think."

I shut my laptop so hard I feared that I'd broken it. That wasn't what I was expecting, and though I could see why Don was pissed about someone being that openly critical of faculty, it's not like I could blame the kid. I had to pretend that the book most of these kids probably read in seventh grade was advanced material.

Backlogging through some of the term papers Mr. Dean had left, my eyes stopped on one particular name. *James*. He was the kid who tried to be snippy because I took his phone. I read the first few sentences of his paper, and I was admittedly stunned. He was playing the dumb card while putting together work like this? Is that what kids had to do to survive at this place?

What had I gotten myself into?

DON

THIS ARROGANT LITTLE SHIT . . . HOW DARE HE COME INTO my school acting like he knows better than we do?

I'd been doing this for fifteen years, and I'd seen the trouble his ilk got up to . . . Smoking in the bathrooms, mirrors on their shoes, starting fights in the cafeteria. His kind didn't care about their education or their peers, only themselves. They had no place here.

Now one of them had a microphone, and I'd be damned if I wasn't gonna record it and bring it right to Principal Sawyer's attention. She'd been far too lax on this, and it needed to be a focus for the safety of the school. She wanted to improve things after last year's bomb scare. Well, this was how you did it—by weeding out the ones with problems they take out on others. My son wasn't gonna get assaulted by some idiot with no future who contributed nothing to this school, or to society itself!

How brave was it to be anonymous? Not at all, I'd say. He knew I'd wring him by the neck and have his ass thrown out of here with the rest of the losers. He *knew*.

That was why he was in hiding. That was why he wouldn't come forward. He knew what would happen to him on my account. Zero-goddamn-tolerance.

". . . just the same way they try to treat our hallways like the Social Darwinists would want. Be liked, popular, do what they want, go to where your parents want you to go to school, but you better not pursue anything in the arts!" that coward said.

"Dog-eat-dog world, boy. Better get used to it now," I responded, echoing what I intended to say when I snatched him myself. And make no mistake—it would be *me* who found him.

"Better not want to act in the theater; that'll just get you working in the coffee shop. Don't pursue philosophy; wouldn't want you to think too much. English? Nobody reads books anymore, why would you want to write them? History? Don't we have enough history? Stop living in the past!"

"Take your own advice, you little clown!" I screamed before accidentally knocking the recorder away from the speaker. Shit, I'd have to cut that part out before I gave it to Principal Sawyer. Wouldn't want her to focus on the wrong person.

"I will find you," I grumbled as I scrambled from my chair to put everything I'd dropped back together. "You can't hide from me for long. You've left a trace somewhere, and I'll find it!"

JESSE

BLOOD TRICKLED INTO THE SINK FROM MY LEFT WRIST. I needed to avoid the person in the mirror staring back at me, for he was not me. He would never be me. I'd never be able to make that person reflect the person I was. It was hopeless.

My eyes drifted despite themselves. Making contact with the steel hazel of my irises found me surprisingly lethargic as I felt the wetness spread. My feminine skin, my stupid chest, my height . . . Oh, god, my height!

I was too short for people to leave me alone as a guy. I looked like a guy, but a feminine one. One too feminine for the fragile masculinity of these Neanderthals who called themselves my classmates. It's revealing both of how they viewed femininity, and of the role that overcompensation for masculinity had on cis boys. It was sick. It was all sick.

"Don't post it online, it might make the bullies feel bad!" the Voice yells. Modified or not, I feel like I'm the only one truly hearing him. The whispers had been prevalent lately, but they were listening. I was hearing what he was saying. "Don't stir the fucking pot, right?"

Right. God forbid we stood up for ourselves. That was worth a double suspension. Be a star, don't be a bully, but if someone bullied you, you'd get in just as much trouble for not wanting to be tortured. It reduced you to their level . . . or saved the school from lawsuits and liability. One of those two; I couldn't figure out which.

LIZ

FINALLY. AFTER TWO AND A HALF STRAIGHT HOURS, THEY were done. This time. Tonight.

Sean gently rubbed my back. I knew he was trying to help, but he wasn't. He was only making it worse. The last thing I wanted was help. Correction: the last thing I wanted was to be seen in this condition.

The Voice must've known what it felt like to be disassociated; he was an anonymous voice speaking out. Most people just passively accepted the shit they were given and went on about their days, counting down how many were left until graduation. It was far harder to take a stand, but even harder to be anonymous.

I'd heard some people refer to the Voice as a coward for not wanting to be seen or identified, but as a teenager, that had to be even more difficult, didn't it? What was it we teenagers wanted more than anything? To be seen. Heard. Understood.

Loved.

The Voice was adored, and either he didn't know,

or couldn't risk opening up about it. He knew he'd disappear or be threatened out of it. The lockdown on which this school had been in the last year left no room for dissent. How very American of them.

Two doors slammed; my parents had retreated to their respective rooms. Sean cringed at the sound, but it barely moved me. It was almost a daily ritual now.

I couldn't go on like this. Nothing was going to make this better, especially Sean's good, but utterly useless intentions. I had to break this off before he got hurt even worse.

MARTHA

MY DARK AND BROODING SON QUIETLY GOT ANOTHER bottle of water from the refrigerator before sitting down at the table. His nose was buried in a book, as usual, and he was being as anti-social as ever.

At the risk of driving him away yet again, I tried to sit down next to my son without startling him. What had happened to him? Where was my cheerful, brilliantly intelligent boy? The intelligent part was still there—I could hardly pry his eyes from books—but on occasion, I'd forget what his voice sounded like. I missed it.

"One of these days, I'm going to get you an e-reader so we can get rid of all these books," I joked, hoping his resistance had waned a bit.

"Mom, not this again," he groaned. Nope, still the same purist he always was.

He rose from his chair, and I gently tried to reach for his hand. My grip was tighter than I meant it to be, and he reacted with shock.

"I wasn't trying to start anything, really," I assured

him. I just wanted to see him smile.

"Then why do we keep having this conversation?" he asked. I wanted to say that it was because it was the only way I could get him to have a conversation at all, but Lionel interjected before I could give more reassurance.

"We don't want you to get left behind, son." His five-o'-clock shadow was dark, matching his wavy hair. Our son was the spitting image of him, including the dark and mysterious expression.

"I'm not going to get left behind because I don't want to read Shakespeare on a screen," our son snapped. Stubborn as his father.

"Print books aren't necessary anymore," Lionel countered.

I sighed and held my breath, knowing what was going to happen next. Lionel loved his son, but didn't understand his obsession with books. I barely was able to get him away from a used book store for under a hundred bucks. "There's no reason to keep filling your room with them."

Shit, we'd lost him tonight. *Here we go again . . .*

"You spend more time with your books than you do with your friends!" I tried to spin it so that it didn't sound like a direct attack, which was how I knew he was taking it. He had such resolve, but was so sensitive on top of it. He felt like everyone critiqued his life and never had any positive reassurance, but we didn't know how to be positive about his constant isolation.

"What friends?" he sarcastically remarked.

He reached for the table to grab his copy of *Hamlet* . . . always *Hamlet* . . . but Lionel made physical contact to stop him, trying to get his attention.

"You lock yourself up in your room all day, you spend your time with books older than your grandparents, and you expect us not to be worried?" he chided.

Moving my head to my hands, I buried it in defeat. I heard my son snatch his favorite book, of which he must've had six copies with different interpretations, and head toward the staircase.

Out of sheer desperation, Lionel went for a Hail Mary. "We don't want you to miss everything, son. You only go to high school once!"

"I hope," he muttered.

"Don't you want to have memories of your youth?" Lionel pressed. "Don't you want to look back and know that you used the time you had well?"

I heard our son's footfalls stop, and I knew he was turning around to give his father the death stare for trying to be the cool dad. "I prefer the characters in books," he answered. I'd gotten that one too many times, and I wished it was sarcasm, but it wasn't.

"He's your son," Lionel laughed. I couldn't help but snicker a bit in response.

"With his father's stubborn streak," I added.

"What are we going to do about this, Martha?" he asked instead of telling me what the answer was for once. It had taken him longer than it had me, but his resolve had finally waned.

"There's not much we can do," I conceded. "It's not like he's getting into trouble. His grades aren't suffering. Do you think maybe we're being too hard on him?"

"Maybe," he replied, his gaze drifting back to the staircase. "I can't help it if I don't want to see him lack the social skills he needs when he goes away to college. He'll never learn to go out and have fun if he's hiding in his room with his books all the time."

I shrugged, not fearing this as much as he did. That was, after all, what I did myself, and how he found me. Turned out all right for somebody. "I understand that, Lionel, but that's how *you* had fun back then. He's not you, he's him. Remember that."

MISS HUNTER

IT WAS MY FIRST FACULTY MEETING, AND I COULD FEEL all the tenured instructors staring at me, as if to ask, *Who let the hippie in?* Principal Sawyer, to whom I'd only been briefly introduced, rose at the head of the long table in her perfectly pressed pantsuit.

"Before we get to today's business," she began, "I'd like to welcome Miss Hunter to Columbus Area High School. Miss Hunter, would you please stand up?"

Dammit, this was embarrassing enough back when I was in high school; I didn't need it now. Regardless, I stood, trying to hide my increasingly red cheeks in the process.

"She's taking over for Mr. Dean," she continued, who is now on indefinite leave, I'm sorry to say. We'll discuss who will take over the English department later in the semester, but for now, Miss Hunter is handling his classes just fine."

"Thank you, Principal Sawyer . . ." I tried to intrude.

"Joyce, please," she politely corrected.

"Joyce . . ." I repeated the name, as if committing it

to my brain like a password. "I only hope to prove no inconvenience to anyone."

"Now," she said, quickly cutting off my formality, "do you have any zero-tolerance reports to file?"

Straight to the point, this one. It felt like camp when I was a teenager when we had to stand against the wall for bed checks like it was the freaking military or something. "No, nothing to report," I responded, with only a tiny bit of zing in my voice.

"I expect to hear from you soon, Miss Hunter," Joyce lectured. "Not just threats, either, but inflammatory arguments, incitement, inappropriate material in an essay . . . Zero-tolerance means anything that might disturb the order of the school."

So official, and so intimidating; it wasn't hard to see how she'd become a person of authority. Her presence alone terrified me.

"And if any faculty are discovered to have been aware of a violation of zero-tolerance policy and don't report it . . ." She narrowed her eyes. ". . . consider it grounds for termination and removal of tenure."

Every back was stiff in their chair by this point. "Now, does anyone have anything to report?"

The air chilled as everyone wondered if they'd be employed, or if they'd missed an allusion to Salinger as a "threat." Taking any risks was obviously not welcome here.

Don, the security guy, stood up ardently. Maybe it was time to find out what all his investigations had produced. He firmly placed a pocket recorder on the table, and it made the young man next to me giggle.

"Wow, Don. What'd that cost you, five dollars?"

Finally, at least there was someone else who saw the absurdity in all of these Thought Police tactics. His plaid shirt and hipster beard should've given it away, but I wasn't ready to assume anyone was on the side of rationality around here.

"This is no time for jokes, Brady," Don growled.

So, his name was Brady. Hmm . . . Maybe I'd have to see if he'd be willing to share lunch duty.

The security guard continued, "We know the troublemakers have to be dealt with, and our job is hard enough without someone making it worse."

"Oh please," Joyce groaned, "please tell me you're not on about the Internet voice guy again!"

"I'm serious," Don insisted. "Has anyone else heard this guy?"

Meekly, I raised my hand, knowing I'd bring his wrath down upon me, but I was habitually honest. Don pointed at me and then moved into my personal bubble. Too close, too close, too close. He stank of too much Old Spice cologne. I couldn't help thinking he used it as a replacement for deodorant. It wasn't working.

I was nothing if not desperate for communal bliss, so I gave it one shot. "Our kids have a choice whether or not to listen to a show about the school. Frankly, I'm surprised any of them think about school when they're not here."

I'd hoped that would be enough to smooth over any tense feelings that would arise from my plea for letting it go. I hoped wrong.

"Thanks for backing me up, Blondie," I heard him mutter.

"I beg your . . ." I began to righteously snap. Who

did he think he was, talking to me like that?

"Enough, Don!" Joyce interrupted "Until this Internet voice does anything other than annoy you out of your primetime crime marathons, I don't want to hear any more about it!"

"You'll be sorry when we see more of those idiots wearing safety pins and nail polish," Don sneered. Great, he was going after the artists. We were never going to get along. "Thought we were rid of that crap ten years ago."

"Oh, no," Brady faux-cried, "we'll be sorry!"

Thank God for him, or I might've quit already.

SEAN

I COULDN'T BELIEVE SHE WAS DOING THIS. HERE. NOW. At school, with everything going on! Desperately, I searched for something happy so I wouldn't start crying in front of everyone.

"So, that's it?" I asked her. "Why are you doing this, Liz?" I'd stood by this girl through everything and tried to be there for her. Why was she getting rid of me? I hadn't done anything wrong!

"Because, Sean," her gorgeous voice quivered in a combination of sadness, and I think fear, "we can't keep doing this with the way things are."

"What, you mean with your parents?"

"Yes, with my parents," she confirmed. "I'm sorry. I can't."

She was breaking up with me over her parents fighting? What kind of reason was that to abandon me? What in the actual fuck?

"You can't what?" I implored. "You're dating me, not them!"

Liz's eyes twitched, and I realized I'd taken it too

far. I always seemed to do that with her, and I never meant to.

"I can't sit there every night, listening to them fighting over every little thing," she sobbed, "knowing we'll probably end up exactly like them someday. Why not get out of it now before it's too late?"

"You mean before you prove them wrong?" I countered uselessly.

"I can't, Sean. Just let me go."

Liz buried her face in her hands and ran away crying. Great, what an amazing way to start the day.

Fighting the urge to cry with all I had, I noticed some kid I didn't recognize in a black shirt, staring at us like we were a play for his entertainment.

"What the hell are you looking at?" I snarled. I didn't want an answer. I wanted my Liz back. That was all I wanted.

He didn't answer. His eyes turned toward a commotion down the hall. Some of the seniors were torturing what I could only assume was another freshman victim. At least it wasn't me they went after anymore.

As I turned back to the voyeur, he walked with authority toward the commotion. *Poor soul,* I thought to myself, *he actually thinks he's going to make a difference. Doesn't he know how it works around here?*

JAMES

THAT KID HADN'T LEARNED HIS LESSON. BETTER HIM than me, at least. I wasn't about to get on Will's radar.

"Looks like the freshman wants to be a princess," he teased.

His views on gender in society were pretty fucked up, but no one was in a place to question him. This poor kid would learn to sink or swim. I'd learned to do the same, and I made myself agree so as not to make myself the next target.

"Looks like maybe he wants a boyfriend," I suggested, dying a little inside. I was in the GSA, for fuck's sake.

"I think you're right, James," Will affirmed at the expense of this poor, young kid whose day we were about to ruin again. "Not too many girls around here are into little sissies like this, right?"

His girlfriend, Veronica, pushed into the circle. Oh, fuck, what was she thinking? "Leave him alone, Will!" she screamed.

Will shoved the kid and turned toward her with fire

in his eyes. Was he going to hit her too? I didn't think I could stand for that. There were some lines you didn't cross, no matter who it was.

"Shut the fuck up, Veronica," he warned her, voice low. "That's the last time I'm going to tell you!"

My blood boiled, but I kept it under wraps.

I tried to grab the kid to get Will's attention away from her. Snatching his left wrist, he cried out like I'd stabbed him.

"I barely touched you!" I snapped, covering the guilt I felt for hurting him. He was barely 100 pounds soaking wet.

Will noticed that his wrist was covered up. He reached for it and the kid panicked. "No, stop!"

Oh shit, was he a cutter? What had we done?!

"What, you playing with the pink lady razors too much?" Will taunted. *Goddammit, Will!*

"Leave him alone," a voice interjected. I knew that voice, but I couldn't quite place it. Turning, I saw that kid who stood up for the nerd the other day. Lucas. Thank god. At least someone had the spine to stop this madness.

Will cleared his throat while glaring at me. Fuck, I knew this was gonna happen. He expected me to take care of him so he could continue with his little guppy.

"Don't you mean 'her'?" Will called back, again clearing his throat and telling me with his eyes that I needed to get in on this or I'd be next.

"What's the matter, hero?" I did my best Will impression in Lucas' direction, regretting it immediately. This kid was stacked under that black shirt he always wore. "Come to save your girlfriend?"

Lucas didn't back down. I was impressed with his fortitude, even though I didn't think even he could make it against Will. Nobody stood up to Will, else they ended up transferring schools.

Lucas' eyes burned into mine. Great, now I had two intimidating people wanting me dead for different reasons. I was a guy without a country.

"If *he* wants to be *her*, that's none of my business, nor is it yours," he countered. I thought of the couple trans kids in the GSA and how disappointed they'd have been with me if they'd seen me in this situation. I doubted I could show my face there again after this. "And whatever he's hiding under his long sleeves in September, what you're probably doing right now isn't helping, so knock it off before you ruin someone else's life."

Fuck, this guy was serious.

"Don't get involved," Veronica pleaded. "They'll never leave you alone!"

Oh, shit.

"That's it, you dumb bitch!" Will predictably screeched. "We're through!"

So were all of us, if something didn't happen.

Will pushed Veronica away from him. Dammit, someone needed to stop this. I saw Lucas' attention turn toward Veronica, who had fallen to her knees, and I saw my chance to save face in Will's eyes.

My knee connected with Lucas' stomach in a way that would knock his breath out but not do any damage, hoping he'd get the hint. But then I heard Will's fist connect with his face.

Lucas dropped to the floor, and this tiny freshman

kid beside me tried to shove me away. He was nothing if not brave. Crazy brave. Stupid brave.

"Oh, look, your girlfriend wants to help," I said, again mimicking Will so I wouldn't hate myself even more. It didn't work.

I shoved the kid down against the wall, hoping it wouldn't get him punched too. "Stay down," I whispered. Lucas didn't listen. He fought to get back up, but several of Will's cronies restrained him.

"There, now they can get married," Will teased. What an asshole.

I caught my own in the reflection on the window, and the guilt stung like a wasp. I'd become just like him. What if he had been doing it to overcompensate too?

"Yeah, it's legal now, right?" I added, trying not to cry.

"Take care, buttercup," Will finished with a snort. Dick.

I walked off with the group, hoping none of them would notice my shame. At least Heather wasn't here to witness that. I'd probably be as single as Veronica was, if she had been. I hoped Will wouldn't tell her. Or Veronica.

Oh, shit. Veronica, please don't tell Heather!

JESSE

FUCK! FUCK! MOTHERFUCKING *FUCK!* WHAT WAS wrong with the people in this school? Why was everyone such a fucking asshole? Why did everyone think I was a guy trying to be a girl?! Goddammit!

At least someone had done something about it. Well, one person and that fuckstick's girlfriend, but it didn't do any good. Then again, what good could they have done? He would've taken it out on me later, regardless.

The guy was bleeding from his mouth, and I saw him wipe his lip with his hand. The dark puddle that dripped onto the floor reminded me of what I left in the sink last night, and I gripped my wrist tightly, hoping he hadn't noticed. But of course he had; he'd shamed that dumb fuck over it.

He knew.

The guy saw the blood on his skin and jumped to his feet quicker than I could react. Was he going to take it out on me too? They always seemed to. I was an easy target. Great morals for the guys who were the focus and representatives of the school, eh?

He reached down to me. I braced for a smack, but surprisingly, the gesture was meant to help me up. He easily pulled me to my feet, and I barely reached his shoulder. How did this guy get taken out? He was huge!

"Thanks for trying." I did my best to hide my dismay. "But they never stop."

"Don't worry about them," he muttered, glaring down the hallway. Maybe he was deliberating following them, but he was gloriously outnumbered. If only we had more on our side.

"What's your name?" he asked after an angry sigh of concession.

"Jesse," I said. No one else knew me by that name outside of my parents, not even the school, but I had to start being honest somewhere. I hoped he didn't ask if I was a girl or becoming one.

I looked back up and saw that his eyes were glued to my wrist. It began to feel hot under the wrapping. "Don't let them make you hurt yourself, Jesse."

He called me by the correct name! But he knew! He knew the worst thing in the world, but it felt so right! Dammit! Why did this have to be so hard?!

"I gotta go," I said, then ran down the hall, hoping he wouldn't follow me. I sprinted past Will's girl, feeling like I should ask if she was okay, but I couldn't bring myself to stop. The longer I was around, the longer people had to ask questions.

VERONICA

MAYBE HE'D LET ME OFF EASY, BUT THAT SON OF A BITCH had still put his hands on me.

Sure, I could tell school security, and they'd probably suspend me for trying to sabotage the football season. I could tell the authorities, but who would believe me? I didn't have any marks to show what he did, and any witnesses were probably just as useless. Save for maybe two.

But one of them ran past me before I was able to ask if he was all right. It was ridiculous that people had to suffer so our school could win football games, but if anyone else accidentally had a nail clipper in their bag, they were treated like a terrorist. Where was the Voice? We needed him!

I considered running after the crowd, hoping Will wouldn't notice me ignoring his parade crashing, but Tall, Dark, and Handsome was still trying to stop the bleeding on his lip. Cute as hell though he was, I wanted to give him the best advice I could. Our eyes met briefly, but his gaze darted to the ground to avoid mine.

He thought I was still on their side, no doubt, and who could blame him?

"You don't want to mess with those guys," I said.

He brushed past me and started walking away. I turned to keep pace with him. "They never change," I added, hoping to get some sort of response beyond the one I probably deserved.

"At least they hit me and not him," he stammered, not breaking his pace.

I stopped. Reaching out was obviously useless. What was the point?

"Wait!" I called out, realizing the shortcoming of our interaction. "What's your name?"

From the end of the hallway, I heard him respond over his shoulder: "His name is Jesse." His steps stopped near the main door. "Make sure he gets to the nurse before they get to him again."

The door creaked open and slammed shut nearly as quickly. I was alone. It was silent.

This was a nice change. So was he.

Whoever he was . . .

LIZ

GOD, I WAS SUCH A BITCH! I HAD LET MY PARENTS RUIN everything! I couldn't wait to get out of this stupid school and never have to think about any of it again!

Finally, the damn bell rang. Another day done, and one day closer to graduation and getting out of this place. I moved toward the exit as fast as I could, and accidentally bumped into someone. Looking up, I saw a pretty blonde girl. Shit, she had to be one of the popular ones. *Please don't attack me, not today!*

"Watch where you're going!" she chastised.

I turned around, completely embarrassed. "I'm sorry, I'm sorry!" I said frantically. "I'm just . . . I . . . I'm sorry."

She smiled, hopefully not before lighting my soul on fire or whatever it was the kids did these days. "Relax, I'm not going to hit you or anything."

Right, like if you were, you'd say so. Why should I trust someone who comes right out and says something like that?

"I just broke up with my boyfriend," I blurted.

"Some kid got punched in the hallway. I'm not taking any chances."

"Some kid?" she responded, confused. Wasn't she there? I could've sworn she was.

Screw this. I didn't need to relate all the details of something I wasn't even involved in. I started to walk away, trying to put myself back together, lest I offend my parents for also having a life that had pain in it.

"Wait, hold on a second!" she called after me.

Great, I thought. I knew it was too good to be true. Girls like me don't get breaks.

"What, change your mind?" I remarked, waiting for a smack across my face. Interestingly enough, it didn't come.

"Do you want to hang out?" she asked, nearly making me swallow my gum in the process. "Maybe I know something that can help you feel better."

Was she propositioning me? Because I was okay with that, if she was.

"Good luck with that. What could you and I possibly have in common?" I said instead, hoping she liked girls who played hard to get.

She smiled. "Have you ever listened to the Voice?"

BRIAN

I SAW THIS POOR, DISHEVELED FUCK CRYING HIMSELF silly on the side of the wall out front. What could his problem possibly be? Did Principal Dickfingers feel him up for shit he didn't have to?

"What's gotten into you?" I inquired as I smacked him on the back, hoping the distraction would derail his outburst.

"Who the . . . ?" he looked up. "Oh, shit, I'm sorry. Is this your spot or something?"

"I have a spot?" This was news, but not some I was willing to argue with. "Cool. Did you claim it for me?"

"No, just . . ." He turned his gaze away, trying not to burst into tears again. I could sense it.

"Just what, dude? Some chick suck your dick and break up with you or something?" Might as well go for the gold, if we're sticking with absurdity.

"Yeah," he replied before realizing what he agreed to. "I mean wait, what?"

"Relax, my friend. I know just the thing. Why don't you come listen to the Voice with me tonight? You know what that is, right?"

"Of course," said, surprising the hell out of me. "I listen every night."

"Me too," I admitted, digging this poor shlub already.

"I'm pretty sure he goes here."

I rolled my eyes. "Of course he does, you Lepton." How else could anyone have that much to say about this shithole if they weren't on the inside of Cell Block 6?

"I don't . . ." he started, then once again shook his head in confusion. "Wait, what?"

"He's been doing the nameless thing for several months," I explained, not even bothering to explain the reference if he didn't get it already. "On the air, no music, no bullshit, a few letters, and he talks until he's done talking." I should know; I was pretty sure I'd been listening to him from the beginning.

"And nobody knows who he is?"

DON

HOW COULD NOBODY ELSE BE TAKING THIS GUY seriously? He was such a threat to the integrity and security of our school. It shouldn't have even been up for debate!

I was walking beside that young idiot teacher, Brady, and hoped I could talk some sense into him at least. "Why won't anyone do anything about this guy?" I asked, hoping his smart-ass demeanor would make him show off for the new English teacher.

"Well, gee, Don," he snarked, "you think a kid who's referred to only as *the Voice* wants anything to do with being outed or identified?"

"What right does someone have to be anonymously provoking the students?" I indignantly demanded. Freedom of speech stopped when security was called into question. Plus, this wasn't a free speech zone, it was my damn school, and my job was to keep someone from doing something stupid. That meant getting rid of the troublemakers, and there was no bigger troublemaker than an anonymous kid who thought he had something to prove.

"I don't see how venting online in his way is any different from the countless passive-aggressive Facebook posts that happen all the time," Brady noted.

But it *was* different. I could feel it in my gut.

And I needed to find the son of a bitch before he proved me right.

JAMES

FUCK . . . WILL WAS FOLLOWING ME HOME AGAIN. WASN'T IT enough that he had to make me act like him in order to survive high school?

"Hey," he called in his normal, brutish manner. "You listening tonight?"

"Listening?" He couldn't possibly mean . . .

"The Voice, dumbass," he teased. "I don't know who he is, but he's really pissed about this school."

"Sounds like someone we should hang out with," I admitted.

JESSE

My house stood empty, desolate, as if no one had been there in days. It was possible that, outside of me, that wasn't entirely inaccurate.

I closed the door behind me, dropping my bag without a care for what was in it. Stupid assignments I'd probably never get to. What was the point? Nobody called me by my real name, anyway, except that guy today.

It was already almost getting dark. I must've taken the long way while staring at the trees. They were the only form of life that didn't make me feel like I was still the stupid girl who didn't know any better. They get it all wrong at school. They think I'm a guy who's trying to be a girl. Can't I just be a guy? Can't I not have my femininity questioned? Isn't it dysphoric enough that I have to deal with it without their goddamn microscope?

At least there was one voice out there, one person willing to speak up for more than those of us who score touchdowns or slam dunks. Him, and the kid who got punched for my sake, though he'd probably beat me up on his own for getting him punched tomorrow. It was a nice thought while I was allowed to have it, anyway.

"THE WORDS 'ZERO-TOLERANCE' ROSE OUT OF THE POST-9/11 paranoia and are now taken as gospel by those who seek to control us," the Voice elegantly explained as I clutched a wad of paper towels against my wrist. Trying to take off my jacket had ripped one of my cuts open, and I was out of Band-Aids . . . not that they would've done any good with cuts like this anyway.

"They claim it's zero-tolerance for weapons, but in the process, they suspend students for fighting back against someone who attacked them. They send kids home for safety pins and knitting needles. Worst of all, they do this while under the false guise of protecting you."

I clutched one of the safety pins I kept in my high pocket, in case I needed to cut again. It wasn't the coolest thing in the world, and even I could admit that, but it was also like having a safety blanket. Feeling the cold metal reminded me I was alive, and having the ability to cut my skin at least meant that sometimes when I hurt, I was doing it to myself. My choice. My decision.

Not like their decision to reject who I was. Fuck them. Fuck them all.

BRIAN

I RECLINED IN POP'S LOUNGE CHAIR. FUCK HIM—HE didn't need it, anyway. Sean, which I'd found out was his name, sat on the couch trying not to look like a kicked puppy. Maybe the Voice could cheer his ass up before he harshed my mellow.

"As you know, I will read your emails if you send them to me at NamelessStateofDenmark@cahs.edu."

That was so badass that he'd managed to get himself a school email address, though I didn't get the Denmark thing. We weren't anywhere near a big city, let alone another country.

"Like *Hamlet,* right?" Sean laughed. I wasn't sure if he was wondering out loud, or looking for affirmation.

"Yeah, *Hamlet,*" I answered. "To be or not to be, and all that."

"Yes, the school's servers are providing me with email privileges without their knowledge or consent," the Voice explained. Lunatic!

"I miss Liz," Sean babbled.

"Cheer up, buttercup." I forced a smile while subtly

telling him not to cry himself to sleep in my house. "She's probably just as upset as you are."

"You think so?" he asked.

I went with it. "Of course. That's what chicks do. They cry for three days after they pretend that they don't give a shit about you."

"Sorry," he mumbled. Good boy. None of that emotional shit here.

"No problem," I told him. "Now shut up. I want to hear the show."

LIZ

HEATHER WAS SO CUTE. I COULDN'T STAND IT.

How had I never noticed this before? I'd always thought of myself as a normal straight girl, and here I was, moments after breaking up a long-term relationship, having the butterflies because a blonde girl was being nice to me.

"Hey," she called as she sat down at the kitchen table with her laptop. "How are you holding up?" She lifted my chin to see my face better. Ohmygod, her touch was electric. I was in so much trouble. I wasn't sure whether to cry or kiss her.

"I'm trying," I lied. Look at those eyes. How could someone have not fallen in love with them already?

"Dear Voice." The Voice interrupted our moment, or at least my moment. This girl was probably straight and laughing at my crushing on her, or she would be if she ever found out. "I think you're a pussy for saying all these things anonymously."

"Fuck that," Heather blurted before covering her mouth. "Sorry, hope that doesn't bother you."

I took a bold step and reached for her hand to assure her. "It's okay," I promised. She didn't pull it away.

Holy shit...

"Why don't you let us know who you are?" he continued as I pretended that was my top priority and not the girl-feels that were pulsating through my body at that very moment. "Ironically sent by someone who didn't leave a name and used an obviously fake email address. Maybe it's that Nigerian prince finally showing up with that money he promised me."

Heather's fingernail gently touched mine. There was no way she'd be doing that if she were just trying to be nice.

Holy shit, holy shit, holy shit, holy shit. Liz, don't screw this up!

MARK

"SINCE YOU SO KINDLY ASKED," THE VOICE SAID IN response to his letter, "anonymously why I'm anonymous . . ." I waited for it while I battled with an orc in the High Gardens. Son of a bitch kept ducking me at every turn. I desperately needed a save point.

"It wouldn't matter if you knew who I was. I'm as nameless in school as I am here, and while you convince yourself that you wouldn't ever treat someone that way, you do. Not even intentionally, really. There are just those you pass . . ."

I was out of arrows. Dammit, the Voice was distracting me again. I mean, his sound was fine, but he was more intense than usual. It was weird not listening only to provide tech and reassurance.

"Every single day, you think you know them, but you can't even recall their name," he elaborated. Damn, if only he knew what it was like to be that faceless nerd in your class . . . Then again, maybe he did. Maybe he was the one who got everything. I thought I was the only one. Maybe I wasn't alone.

"But you've had at least one class with them, right? Perhaps they're in your homeroom, sitting there every day, silently, wistfully waiting for the meaningless period of checking attendance to be over."

I didn't mind homeroom too much. Gave me time to catch up on my new fantasy novel, but I got what he was saying. It made us come to school earlier to be accounted for, and I couldn't think of anything beyond that reasoning.

"Maybe they're attempting to fight through the morning fog of being at the Mind Correctional Facility that early," he snapped.

Ouch. Not a fan of public education, apparently. That shouldn't have surprised me as much as it did.

"I mean, they don't even offer us coffee," he added. There he was, always coming in quick with a joke or to light up your smoke. That was the Voice I knew and loved.

VERONICA

I CHECKED OVER MY BRUISED WRIST FROM WHERE WILL had gripped me earlier. Unbelievable that he thought that was acceptable behavior, but then again, when has he ever had to deal with any consequences for being an asshole?

The Voice was on his game, and even though his voice was altered, it comforted me to know that someone was willing to stand up against this bullshit, even if he couldn't do it visibly. Something had to be done before someone got hurt, and a lot worse than I or that cute guy did today.

"So many of us feel alone—invisible, even," he finally continued.

Oh, shit. Not you too! You sound so intelligent, so amazing; who wouldn't want to be with a guy like that?

"We're surrounded by people all the time, facing the same direction as the Sage on a Stage, dispensing the pre-approved material for that particular day."

I hadn't looked myself in the mirror yet. I couldn't, not with what I'd allowed myself to become over the last few months. Will was a monster, and I'd been an enabler. It was only a matter of time before he crossed the line.

Maybe there was someone out there better for me. I really wished I'd gotten that guy's name. Even though he'd gotten punched, anyone willing to put themselves on the line for someone getting beat up was all right by me. It'd be nice if I'd been strong enough to stop it all the other times it happened when Will did it, but alas, I'd been too afraid.

"Not wanting us to explore anything, not wanting us to think critically, not wanting anything outside the box because that might socially isolate us. They say they don't want others thinking we're weird, but who fucking cares?"

I slammed my fist against the bed. Ouch! Dammit, that wasn't the best idea. But he was right, as usual. Why did we live in such fear of being ostracized? And why did so many people accept it?

"How do we not feel weird when we can stay silent the entire day and nobody notices?" he asked, and I tried to answer him despite the fact he couldn't hear me.

"I'm always here," I told him. "I'm always listening."

"How do we not feel weird when we know better what's out there, but saying it can get us detention or a suspension? When did knowing things become frowned upon in the state of education?"

Since football players started making the school money, I thought before collapsing back onto the pillow. I'd never find a guy like this. He probably didn't even really exist the way I perceived him. I bet he was playing a part and nothing more to stir up controversy.

But I needed to find out who he was. So badly.

I heard Mom open the door, and I knew what we were in for. Another check-up.

"I know you really liked this boy, but there will be others," she said as she sat down next to me on the bed. Wow, that wasn't what I was expecting.

"I never said there wouldn't be," I answered, hoarse from the crying earlier. Might as well let her think it was because of the breakup and not because of . . .

"I hate seeing you in pain, that's all," my mother explained further. I wanted to hug her so badly, but I'd pushed affection so far out of my mind that I couldn't find the words to thank her for it. I was hoping she'd see it anyway.

"Right," I groaned, "gotta put on the happy face, gotta smile so that Prince Charming will come save the helpless damsel in distress."

"You're not a damsel, Veronica," she replied. *Thank you so much, Mom.* I wanted to hug her and tell her I loved her, but I couldn't. Not here. Not now. "I don't want you to be hurting like this, that's all."

Thanks, Mom, I thought sincerely, but I couldn't say it. Stupid, dumb teenager brain.

"I won't," was all I mustered. So not sufficient, but she took the hint that I didn't really want. Gently rubbing my leg for a second, she left, checking on me before she started to close the door.

"I don't know what it is you're listening to all the time," she added before completing her exit, "but it's starting to worry me."

"It's nothing to worry about," I assured her.

"If you say so," she answered, which was code for *I disagree, but I'm done arguing.* So be it. That was enough for now.

As I turned my headphones back up, the Voice came back to me, the only one that spoke the truth. "Even those you think are untouchable, invincible, surrounded by all the love you could ever wish for, they're hurting too. They just hide it the most, and they overcompensate with aggression."

Will. It had to be Will he was talking about, which meant . . .

No, it couldn't be . . .

JAMES

WILL WAS PRESSING THE BARBELL OFF THE BENCH PRESS, as usual. He had to do that one more so everyone could see how awesome he was. He'd probably do it with cheerleaders if he wanted any chicks around during his workout, but he gave them bad looks for coming to the gym at all. Typical douche.

The Voice continued his show through the speakers. Will's dad owned the place, so it wasn't like anyone was going to question his listening material.

"They lash out at others because they don't know how to handle the emptiness they're feeling inside," the Voice explained.

Too fucking close to home, brother.

"I'm not a fan of the idea that mean actions come straight out of nowhere. It comes from a place of pain that they've been told they're weak if they acknowledge."

Will dropped the barbell with a thud, and I heard a thunderous voice from a hidden room. "Don't drop the fucking weights, faggot!" it screamed. "Pick it back up before I teabag your mother."

Will begrudgingly lifted the weight again and placed it on the rack, muttering to himself.

Timing, holy shit. Sometimes it was really a coincidence beyond explanation.

JESSE

I LAY CURLED UP IN THE BLANKET I'D HAD SINCE I WAS five, listening to the echo of the wind brushing branches against my house. It used to make me think monsters were attacking, but I knew the truth. The real monsters were in my school, and worse, in my own head.

"I'm sick of the security officers brushing me along and searching my backpack, but if I resist, I'll get suspended, or worse. What can I do about them violating my rights? Signed, A Longtime Listener."

The cold metal gleamed in the light from the only source; my computer screen. Something had to be done about this. Somebody had to make the Voice's words a reality.

JAMES

WILL AND I WERE AT A DINER, SITTING ACROSS FROM ONE another while he glared at his plate of eggs. I didn't even expect him to come out this late, but there he was, still staring intently at the speakers as if the Voice was going to come out of the screen and smack him himself. I'd never seen Will so affected by something anyone said. Honestly, I wasn't sure if it was the Voice or his father who had done this to him.

"More coffee?" the waitress asked me.

"Sure." I slid my cup for her to pour. That was nice, always keeping an eye on it despite me not spending more money. It was good to have a place to go without having to deal with other issues.

"Yes, it's true," the Voice continued, Will tapping his fingers anxiously, "if you resist some stranger with a hard-on for tight clothes, wearing a badge like he's a fucking cop, you're seen as the problem, perhaps even a terrorist."

Yeah, right! Even with my connections to the security department, it was infuriating how they made every kid feel like a criminal. Then they'd be surprised that if you treated a kid like one, they behaved like one. Funny.

"Maybe they think you're going to shoot up the place with that stash of pot you've got in the secret compartment of your backpack. Better call the bomb-sniffing dogs for that one. That nickel bag just cost the taxpayers three grand. For your protection."

Will buried his head in his hands. Emotions, coming from someone I'd previously thought dumb and impervious to them? I wasn't sure how to handle it.

"Carry a copy of the Bill of Rights with you so that they can literally take your rights away when they find it," he suggested. "Maybe comment on the paranoia it must take to search every student at a school where there's never been any violence."

Fuck, that was deep. Too deep. Too close.

THE VOICE

"THEY DON'T WANT YOU TO DO ANYTHING THAT DRAWS attention to yourself," I clarified, leaning in even closer to the mic than usual. "But that's what you have to do—draw attention. If you draw attention, then they're in the spotlight too. That's the last place they want to be."

Boy, didn't I know from personal experience, especially after how things had gone today . . .

"The last thing anyone forcing themselves on you wants," I muttered, thinking of that asshole I dealt with, "is to be seen doing the thing they claim is so right and just. Then they'll be forced to confront what is already clear to me, and I'm sure to some of you."

I prepared for the final slam, the zinger . . . what my speech professor would call a clincher. "They are unjust, they aren't right, and they don't want to acknowledge it. Shine a light in the darkest corners, and you'll always find someone in authority waiting there, holding someone else down under the triumphant banner of safety."

Clicking off the connection, I let it fade into their

memories. I doubted anyone seriously cared about what it was I had to say, but I couldn't help but notice more people talking about it than ever.

Sitting up from my office chair, I noticed there was still blood on my shirt from where that guy punched me. I didn't realize it had stained my clothes too. Goddammit. I lifted the shirt over my head and collapsed on my bed, my jaw clenched. I was usually better than that—better about having my own back and not blindly walking into a stupid situation . . .

But normal stupid situations didn't have *her* there.

Her, the prettiest girl I'd ever seen, but I constantly kept my head down around her because of who she was with. Now she wasn't with him. Was I an asshole for thinking about taking my shot now that she was free? Would that classless shitgibbon come after me for going after what he saw as his slice? And did she even know I existed?

Fuck it, these were questions to answer another day. Scanning my bookshelves for something new, my finger stopped at Shakespeare's sonnets. What can I say? I wasn't used to having romance in my heart, and I wondered if #38 would resonate with me now that I knew she'd at least seen me, even if it was while I was getting my ass kicked.

"How can my muse want something to invent when thou dost breathe?" I read aloud. Who needed a muse with a knockout like that noticing I existed?

Fantasy, pure fantasy is all it was. Nobody ever noticed me at that place. Why would she be any different?

But I hoped, despite myself. Sometimes, hope is all

that keeps us going. Better than this life. Beyond this life. Anything else seemed appealing by comparison.

"Stop being depressing, Lucas!" I yelled at myself, trying to get rid of my negative feelings. No time for those. For once, I had something to cling to, even if it was something that would never come true.

Tomorrow, I would try to talk to her, just once. What was the worst that could happen?

DON

FINALLY, I GOT THE BASTARD. I'D KNOWN IT WAS HIM ALL along! Who else could've been stirring up a ruckus other than him? Kid was making my job difficult every single day, and now I had him.

I dragged him toward his favorite place—the office—yet again. Knowing I had to make sure that he stayed this time, I wasn't about to let him wander his punk ass off.

"Get off me, man!" he screamed. "I didn't do anything!"

"Sharp objects on your person, potential weapon," I informed the creep. "Zero-tolerance policy, Dracula." I've been waiting to say that to him for months.

"Sounds like your wife also has a zero-tolerance policy," he snapped back like the miscreant he was. "You need to get laid, or do you get off on being the Thought Police, you poser?"

That was it. I didn't even know what he meant by that, but it didn't matter. Seeing one of the safety pins on his stupid jacket, I ripped it right from its denim. See if he insulted me again, 'cause next time, I'd make it worse.

"You asshole!" he shouted.

Thank you very much, you idiot. "Get out. You're suspended for the rest of the day," I delightedly told him. "I've got more important business to deal with than the likes of you."

I left him standing there in absolute disbelief. *That's right, you don't have anything smart to say now, do ya?*

The doors opened, and I slammed my tape recorder right on the principal's desk. I was on a roll, and even her negligence wasn't going to stop me today.

"Don, I don't need any more of this right now," she started to protest, but I wasn't listening. It didn't matter. She needed to hear what I'd caught this guy saying.

"Maybe they think you're going to shoot up the place with that stash of pot you've got in the secret compartment," the criminal said. Why was I the only one who was concerned about this type of behavior and how it affected this school? Maybe I should be principal and see how that goes.

I hit the stop button, and glared right at her. Nobody had any excuses to not hear it now. "Drugs, violence, and rebellion," I said with disgust. "That's what he's bringing into this school, Principal Sawyer. This Internet guy has caused nothing but trouble for everyone who works here, and he's going to corrupt the minds of the good students who are listening to him."

That had to do it. Even given her policies of apologies and non-action, she couldn't be that naïve.

"What about the not-so-good students?" she asked,

for some reason changing the subject to the troublemakers.

"The hell with those losers and what they think," I argued back with a grin. "I'm concerned for the ones worth saving."

"Very diplomatic of you," she sarcastically remarked. Dammit, time to turn it up a notch. I still hadn't gotten through to her.

I slammed my hands down on the desk hard enough to shake its contents, or at least the pens.

"This kid is making ambiguous references to school violence. Doesn't this school have a goddamn zero-tolerance policy?" I reminded her. After all, I was the one who convinced her to institute it in the first place.

She stood up, her expression changing, clearly showing that she'd been affected by my words. "I'll look into it, Don," she conceded. Victory!

I rose to meet her glare of defeat and told her straight to her face: "Thank you for finally listening to me . . ."

You dumb bitch, I should've added before I turned and walked away.

"Oh, Don?"

Great, what did she want now? I turned my head as little as I could.

"Yes, Principal Sawyer?" I sarcastically answered, as if I were a kid in detention or something.

"Don't ever barge into my office and take that tone with me again," she bitched. Figures. Probably hadn't changed her tampon that day. "Do I make myself clear?"

"Crystal clear," I replied, rolling my eyes. Crazy woman doing a man's job—she deserved what she got.

JAMES

Miss Hunter started passing us books by rows. I was quite confused, as I didn't remember anything in the syllabus today about a new book to read.

"Isn't this a movie?" that Neanderthal, James, asked.

"It is, but it was a book first," she responded, unfortunately not adding that he'd probably never seen a book before.

"I don't remember seeing this on the syllabus," I offered, and it was true. I kept track of those in every class to make sure we followed them to the letter. No surprises.

"It's not, but the syllabus is always subject to change," she replied.

I was about to protest, but Lucas stood up and walked to her. Maybe he was going to do it for me. That'd be nice; he was way bigger than me, anyway.

"You can have this one back," he grumbled as he handed her his copy. "I already have it."

"Of course you do." James pissed on him like the animal he was. "You and your girlfriend probably read it together, right?"

"That's quite enough," Miss Hunter snapped.

Lucas turned around to face him. He was as big as James was, if not bigger. I liked his chances when it wasn't a cheap shot, but guys like that rarely play fair.

"Well, it does help that we're both actually able to read," he said with a grin.

Thank you, Lucas! I've been wanting to say that for years!

"Keep it up with that big boy talk," James taunted. "We can go teach you another lesson in the hallway right now."

"This ends now, or you'll both be in Principal Sawyer's office!" Miss Hunter yelled. Of course, zero-tolerance logic. Someone stands up for themselves, so better punish both equally.

"That's all right," James responded, reclining in his chair. "My Dad will get me out."

"Oh, just shut up already, James," his girlfriend, Heather, groaned. How did someone like her put up with a guy like that, anyway?

"Getting you out of an assault charge?" she loud-whispered at him. "That's a tall order for a school security officer, isn't it?"

Wait, *that* was who he was? That was who the security guy was? No wonder James got away with everything! No favoritism there whatsoever, eh?

James' smile faded and he returned to his normal, upright position.

"I suggest you and your friend don't attack any more of my students," Miss Hunter warned. "For your own good."

Badass! I take back what I thought about you, Miss Hunter!

James shot a death glare at Lucas, who couldn't have cared less, judging by his expression. Someone else was looking at him too. Veronica, Will's ex, was giving him the eyes. Interesting development there.

"This book will probably be controversial to some of you, but I assure you, it's a necessary read at your age," she explained. "Even if you've seen *The Perks of Being a Wallflower*, I want you to read it by Monday."

The collective groans sounded throughout the room. Typical high school students.

"You want us to read the entire book that quickly?" Heather complained.

"It's not that long," I said, trying to help. "You'll get through it in no time."

"Of course you will," James interjected against my will. "It's not like you have anything to do."

Asshole.

"It's not a long book," Miss Hunter repeatedly, steering the conversation back her way. "I'm sure your social lives will manage to deal without you for the few hours it'll take. Hopefully, it might reach some of you."

"Yeah, right," James argued again, cementing his place as the village idiot. "When has a book ever done that?"

Seriously, dude? I've got some right now I could . . .

Before I offered my own examples, Lucas tossed a book onto James' desk.

James read the title out loud as if he'd never heard of it. *"Hamlet?* What the hell is this?"

"A book that changed the world," Lucas snarked,

making eyes back at Veronica in the process, "and a lot of people in it."

Miss Hunter cleared her throat. "Lucas?"

"Yes?"

"I'm going to have to send you home for the day," she regretfully informed him.

"For what?" he protested.

"What you just did there could be seen as incitement," she explained. "Due to the zero-tolerance policy, I have to report it, or I could lose my job."

What a bunch of bullshit. This zero-tolerance policy shit was riddled with favoritism at best, and was plain fucking stupid at worst.

"I suppose physical assault is conducive to school activities, but suggesting the reading of classic literature is the bringer of chaos? Words, words, words . . ." he muttered, the reference to the book going over almost everyone else's head.

"I'm sorry, Lucas," she said again. "I'm only doing what I've been asked to."

Lucas stormed out of the room, slamming the door shut behind him, and quite loudly at that. Who could blame him? He gets beat up, and then gets sent home for tossing a book on someone's desk?

The bell rang, and everyone else left. I stayed to ask more about the changes in the syllabus, but before I could, I saw James return to the room. He grabbed the copy of *Hamlet* he'd left on his desk, glared at Miss Hunter, then retreated a second time. Then Miss Hunter also left without noticing I needed to speak to her.

Well, that was fun. Is it college yet?

LUCAS

"Seems yours truly has been making some waves within the sacred halls of Columbus Area High School," I began. No introductions necessary. They were a mere formality at this point. "I've heard our security officer, the ultimate lord and protector of the Columbus High Universe, apprehended an unsuspecting kid believing it was me. Profiling for the win."

I said this in a joking manner, but in truth, it was quite terrifying. The fact that the school was now resorting to hunting people down for using their freedom of speech just because they didn't like what we said, off-school property and during non-school hours, was beyond any Orwellian analogy I could manage to come up with.

"Someone speaks their mind," I continued, "off school property, outside of school hours, and those in power feel they have the right to police our discussions." That was pretty much what was in my head, though I'd definitely thought it better. If only I didn't have a brain-to-mouth filter of stupid.

"Are you seeing this yet? Are any of you paying attention as to what is wrong with this situation?"

JAMES

SITTING IN THE USUAL DINER WHERE WILL AND I pretended to do homework, I struggled through this book that Lucas had thrown at me. I tried to hide my curiosity, but I couldn't help it. I wasn't going to pretend to be an idiot forever just for Will's sake.

I felt him staring at the book cover, so I tried to tune it out and concentrate, but it was difficult. It seemed like it was poetry, but written as people would speak it. What the hell? It was pretty, but I didn't understand what a lot of it meant.

"Since when are you into Shakespeare?" Will asked.

"Shut up," I instructed, "I'm trying to understand what he's saying." Holy shit, did I just tell Will to shut up? I was so dead.

Will stood up, and I knew what I was in for. I waited for his fist to come crashing down on the side of my head, but instead, he slid into the booth next to me as the waitress refilled our coffee.

"What the hell are you doing?" I demanded.

"Try reading it slower," he offered. "The language is

old. Give yourself a chance to understand it."

I stared at him for several seconds. I couldn't believe this was the same guy who pretended to not know anything at school. Maybe we had that in common and were playing off each other because we thought we were supposed to, or something.

"You know this stuff?" I finally asked.

He looked at me almost expectantly. "Of course I do."

Yes, Will. You, the guy who made me beat up someone who was sticking up for your girlfriend. Of course you knew Shakespeare. What was I thinking?

LIZ

SHE WAS HERE WITH ME, SHE WAS HERE WITH ME, HOLY-holy-holy shit, she was here with me!

Some of the students had taken to hanging out at school whenever the Voice came on. Naturally, Sean was one of them, though I think he came because he thought he'd see me, but here I was, with Heather. Was this even real life?

My gaze drifted back toward him, but he seemed distracted by the show going on. That goth guy had hooked up his laptop to a pair of DJ speakers.

Heather's hand accidentally brushed against mine, and I shuddered, worried I'd offended her and ruined everything. Not this, not already! The hottest girl in the school seemed to like me, and I wasn't sure what to do about it.

"Would you two just give up and fuck already?" I heard the goth guy yell. I thought he meant me and Sean, but Sean didn't pay it any mind. Heather, on the other hand, blushed and looked at me through dewy eyes. Her hand touched mine, not accidentally this time, and suddenly her lips were on mine.

Time stopped, and even the cosmos stopped spinning, just for a moment. Our lips parted, and I knew once and for all that the reason I couldn't commit to Sean was because . . . I was gay. The second I kissed Heather, I knew it for a fact. That explained why I never could make Sean understand me, despite him really doing nothing wrong. Oh, good god, my parents were going to love this one.

"I've got another email here," the Voice said, breaking through our little moment. For once, I was disappointed to have him bring us back to reality. But it was a nice change, nonetheless.

"I'm sick of being attacked in school because I don't fit in anywhere," he said, reading from the email. "I try to go about my day without bothering anyone . . ."

JESSE

I HUGGED MY PILLOW. WHAT ELSE COULD I DO? HE WAS reading my letter aloud.

VERONICA

EVEN IF THIS WAS A FAKE VOICE HE WAS USING, WHICH I was certain it was, I could hear it trembling through the distortion. I wanted to reach through the screen and hug him, and whoever sent him this letter as well.

Such pain in this world. Why do we keep doing this to ourselves?

"I don't know how to make the pain stop," he continued. "I feel like there's no way out. I envy you being you, I envy you being the Voice, because that's better than what they call me everyday."

Poor kid. I wished I knew which one of the ones it was that Will likely tormented, but there were too many to recollect.

Glancing in my mirror, I felt awash in guilt and shame. So many times that I could've done something to help, and didn't. Things needed to change, and I needed to do something about this before something bad happened . . . if it hadn't already.

LUCAS

WHAT THE HELL WAS THIS? WHY WOULD SOMEONE SEND this to me? Was it a prank? Was someone really so lonely that they had to reach out to an anonymous voice in the dark? This wasn't right, and it made me even angrier at the school as I read the email.

"It's a tough spot to be in," I managed before I sniffled and teared up a bit. "And sad to say, I know exactly where you're coming from. Hell, some of you see me every day and don't even realize it. The only reason you know I exist is because you hear me on this show, but you'd never know it was me."

That was the best bone I could throw to Brian, who was likely under Deputy Don's investigation right now. The administration needed to at least know it wasn't so obvious, and it helped to ease my own guilt.

MISS HUNTER

COULD THIS BE SOMEONE IN ONE OF MY CLASSES? I HAD A feeling I might know who it was, but I didn't dare ask.

"We're all hurting, and we're all trying to reach out to someone, anyone who will listen," the Voice continued gently.

I'm listening, I wanted to say. *And I know many others are too. You have a voice, kid. Use it.*

PRINCIPAL SAWYER

HONESTLY, I DIDN'T KNOW WHAT THE BIG FUSS WAS. DON made it sound like the masked vigilante from *V for Vendetta* was talking about re-enacting one of its most iconic scenes, with our school playing the role of Big Ben. This sounded like kids talking about their problems when they thought adults weren't listening.

Or, in other words, what everyone but Don probably went through during their own childhoods. Some of the faculty seemed to have forgotten that they were in high school once too.

"But there are those who take it out on others," the Voice elaborated. "There are those who want you to feel pain so they don't have to for a while. If they break someone else, they forget that they're broken."

Sounded like he had Don's number, all right.

LUCAS

I STOOD, CRYING WITHOUT BEING ABLE TO HIDE IT anymore. This was such fucking bullshit, that we had a society that allowed this to happen to some of the kids in our school only trying to make it through the day. Such. Fucking. Bullshit.

"And god fucking forbid if you stand up for yourself," I yelled through my tears, "because you'll get suspended or expelled for daring to say, 'I'm not taking this shit anymore!' They tell us to be ourselves and to stand up to bullies, but they don't want us to actually do either of those things, do they?"

JESSE

I LOST MYSELF IN TEARS AS HE RESPONDED TO MY LETTER. I knew it—there was no actual way out, was there? I had to take matters into my own hands.

"They want you to suck it up, to suffer through this," he screamed, "because it's all going to be a distant memory someday, right? Bullshit! This is your life!"

And it was time to take mine back.

BRIAN

THERE HAD TO BE A DOZEN KIDS HERE NOW, AND I doubted any of them knew who I was. Sean had only drifted to me because I was the only one there to listen to his whining ass. I think it gave him some comfort to know now that his girlfriend had left him because she was a lesbian, not because she hated him. Hopefully that would at least get him to stop eating all my peanuts.

"Stand up for yourself!" the Voice screamed. I shook my fist in approval. He was really on fire tonight. "Tell them you're not going to let them be the cause of your fucking therapy bills in your forties! This pain, it doesn't go away, and it doesn't make it okay that they're getting away with it, even if it isn't completely their fault!"

Sean was crying next to me, but I was sure it was over the Voice's words and not over his lost cause of an ex. Glancing down a few feet away, I saw the two lovebirds crying in each other's arms as well. My arms were still lonely, as they probably would stay as long as I was here in this shithole, but for once, I felt like someone out there knew. Someone out there understood. Someone out there cared.

The Voice.

"Your scars will not heal, and their actions will continue into the adult world."

Explained Don Fuckface, anyway. A bully all grown up, still bullying kids to this day.

MARK

SOMEONE WAS TRYING TO FIND HIM, BUT HAD NO IDEA what they were up against. I could fight this code without even pausing my game.

"You don't have to take this," the Voice said.

No, we don't.

LUCAS

"MAKE THEM HEAR YOUR VOICE! DON'T BE IGNORED anymore! Don't let them take away your name!"

BRIAN

ANOTHER MORNING, ANOTHER GROUP OF DOUCHEBAGS to deal with. I wondered what Dickhead Don was going to come up with today.

At least I was in my usual spot: the stairwell at the west corner of the school. No one bothered me there, even though everyone knew where I was. I liked it that way. Suited my needs just fine.

Except this morning, someone else was approaching me. Not Don, which was a pleasant change, but that chick Liz was hanging out with last night. What the hell did *she* want?

"You lost?" I asked her.

"I think it . . ." she started, then stammered. Her face flushed crimson.

"Go ahead, spit it out," I encouraged.

"I want to thank you," she concluded.

"For what?"

"For helping Sean," she began, "and for . . ."

"Yes?"

"For helping me realize who I was."

I shrugged, even though it meant a lot to hear something other than a criticism for a change. "Don't get all sentimental on me now." I played it off as cool as I could. "Couldn't have done it without your girl."

"I guess, I mean . . ." She stammered again. "I didn't expect this . . . from you."

"Well, I . . ." I started to respond, but then I saw Don making his daily beeline for me. "What's the matter, Chief?"

Without saying anything, he grabbed me by the jacket, nearly tearing the damn thing off. "Hey, what the hell!" I protested.

"You stay away from my son's girlfriend, you useless waste of space!" he screamed.

Wait, what? This chick was . . .

"Don, stop it!" Heather protested. "I came up to him! And James isn't my boyfriend anymore. I don't even have a boyfriend!"

"Yeah, right," Don condescended. "He seduced you, probably to take you off to his cult or something."

Don started to pull me away, and I stripped off my jacket to avoid his clutch. Before I could get away though, he was on me again.

"I'm going to make sure you're expelled from this campus!" he threatened. "You're a waste of education!"

Shit, he wasn't kidding around this time! "Get your hands off me!" I yelled, more panicked than I expected to be. What got up his ass today? And how the fuck was this legal?

"Not so tough now, are ya?" he mocked. Fuck this guy. Seriously, fuck . . . this . . . guy.

Someone tugged on Don's coat arm. "Let go of

him!" a voice instructed. That had to be that James douchebag. This guy's son. Great, just what I needed: a family affair.

But anyone could say anything else, a crack sounded, followed by a release of my jacket.

I turned in time to see James crash to the ground. Heather knelt next to him as he grabbed his temple, then looked up at Dumb Fuck Don. "What the hell is the matter with you?" she demanded.

A crowd started gathering. This was making me extremely uncomfortable, but at least I'd have witnesses this time. "I'll deal with you next," he muttered.

"What, like you deal with your own kid, you fucking psycho?" I hissed. This was fucking disgusting, and if I was gonna get hit or expelled, I was taking him with me. Someone had to be recording this, after all.

"What the hell is going on here?" another female voice intruded. Was that the new lady? Miss Hunter? Before I could do anything about it, Don had me by the back of the neck on the jacket this time, nearly choking me. What the fuck?

"Release that student at once!" she exclaimed. "You have no right to . . ."

"It's my job, Blondie," Dickhead retorted. "Go back to grad school!"

A pant suit appeared in front of me. Thankfully, the principal was here. And that was definitely the first time that thought had ever crossed my mind.

"Calm down, both of you," she demanded. He didn't release his grip. Fuck, what did it take to get this guy to listen?

"Send this annoying grad student home, Principal

Sawyer!" Don was giving orders to the principal now. How quaint.

"He's putting his hands on students!" Miss Hunter contended. "How can this possibly be legal?"

Good fucking question, Ace!

"Miss Hunter," the principal instructed, "take the rest of the day off. You're in no right mind to be teaching."

"Are you serious?" both of us responded simultaneously. Of all the people in this situation, the principal was sending *Miss Hunter* home?!

Principal Sawyer didn't miss a beat. "Zero-tolerance policy," she explained. "It was expressed to you very early on. Leave immediately, or consider yourself suspended."

Miss Hunter's heels clicked away before she got in deeper. Dickhead, still nearly tearing off the neck of my jacket, yelled after her, "Consider staying at home from now on!"

"Unhand that student, or I'll press charges!" Principal Sawyer demanded.

Finally. About fucking time, lady!

Don didn't let go right away, but finally released. I did my best to be cool, despite how much I was shaking.

"Dry-clean only," I snarked. "I'll send you the bill, asshole."

He reached for me again, but the principal stood in his way. The crowd started to disperse, as apparently the interesting part was over. Glad it didn't end in me bleeding on the floor like Don probably wanted.

"Don, I know what you've been trying to do . . ." the principal started.

"But you just stopped me from—"

"I've been looking into your activities," she said, cutting him off. "Thanks to the suggestion of students playing some of the Voice's recordings . . ."

"Not you too, that son of a bitch . . ."

"He has shined a light on some of your particular activities," Principal Sawyer elaborated. "Singling out students and taking things to an extreme with them."

You mean like grabbing them by the neck like a goddamn cat, Principal Sawyer? Like that?

"I've only done what is best for the school," he huffed.

"In light of this, I have no choice but to suspend you indefinitely."

"But I . . ."

"Leave my school now, or I'll have you removed," she insisted.

"You're going to believe some anonymous criminal over your own head of security," Don cried.

"Keep talking, Don," Principal Sawyer said coolly. "How'd you like to be arrested? You're now on private property, and you are not a student or faculty, so you're trespassing. Get out, now!"

Dickhead finally got the message and turned back on us as he left, screaming, "You'll regret this!"

Someone around here fucking did something right. Took 'em long enough!

VERONICA

THERE HE WAS—TALL, DARK, AND HANDSOME, TRYING TO pretend like he had no idea what was going on in the world or what he was doing to it. His humility somehow made him more attractive, especially since he took a punch for someone he didn't know to live up to his own principles. It's hard to find that anywhere, let alone in high school.

I approached slowly as to not scare the poor guy away. He probably still though no one knew, but I did. I'd heard every show he'd ever done, and even though he disguised his voice, his speech pattern made it obvious. Hearing him snark at James gave it away. The *Hamlet* reference in his email address only confirmed it. So cute.

I finally got close enough to squeak out, "I know it's you."

Bless his heart, he tried not to give himself away, but sometimes you know by looking in their eyes. I knew right then, the second he turned around, that not only was he the Voice, but that I was falling for him.

How could I not? He was the only one I could talk to anymore, and I'd never even said anything to him!

"You know *what* is me?" Lucas said, gracefully covering his own embarrassment. This guy couldn't be less like Will if he tried. I didn't know why I put up with that for so long. Will who?

Just look at me again, just speak to me in the voice—the real you, the true you. Speak to me, breathe, talk, damn you! Talk!

"I know you're the Voice," I elaborated.

He shuffled his feet and looked down at the ground. Oh, dear, how had he not given himself away to anyone else? He had no poker face whatsoever!

"I don't know what you're talking about," he muttered, trying to walk away.

I didn't budge from his path. *Be strong, Veronica. Don't let his scent get to you . . .*

Ohmygod, his scent! He wasn't drenched in Axe body spray. How unbelievably refreshing . . .

Dammit, Veronica, focus!

"I'm not going to tell anyone, but don't deny it to me. Your email address is a *Hamlet* reference, same book you tossed at James," I explained, hoping this would put him at ease, but he didn't drop his mask.

"Second-most written about book in the world," he said before adding, "hardly obscure."

"But then you talk about being in fights in the hallway and standing up for those who feel invisible right after you tried to do the same in person," I suddenly gushed, an infodump pouring all over him after the weeks of buildup of the dam in my system. It was like meeting a hero, but he was a real person. *God,*

Veronica, stop making an idiot of yourself!

"Nobody else has put it together, at least that I know of, but I've been listening since you went on. I know why you remain anonymous, I really do, but please . . . let me be a part of it."

He tried to turn around, but I still wouldn't budge this time. I'd been planning this for too long to give up now without breaking through his stubborn resistance.

"Why would you want anything to do with me?" he asked. The question caught me off guard.

I gently put my hands on his shoulders and stared into his eyes. I've been waiting to do that for so long, and at that moment, I swear I forgot my own name.

"I want to know you," I admitted. "I want to be around you, and I want to learn who you are. I believe in you, I've listened to all your words, and now I want to know the person behind the Voice."

I realized I was gripping him way too hard, and I released, hoping I hadn't unnerved him. "I promise you, your secret is safe with me."

When I embraced him, he hugged me back. I didn't know if it was polite or genuine, but it didn't matter. He was always rather cautious unless he was behind a microphone, as far as I could tell, so I didn't take that personally. Once again, it was a nice change from the aggressive oaf I was used to.

"Are you feeling better, Jesse?" I heard him ask, and I flipped around quickly to see the poor kid. I hadn't gotten the nurse. Fuck, I'd let him down again!

His face, red and damp, spoke volumes. He barely turned his head up high enough for me to see it, let alone Lucas, but it was obvious he was distraught.

"Thanks," he sputtered, "for what you did the other day with those guys in the hall."

"I'm sorry I couldn't do a better job standing up for you," Lucas replied.

Jesse turned away, remaining still, as if hearing something off in the distance.

"Jesse?" Lucas prompted.

"You're the only one who ever has," he finally answered, "and I'm grateful. But you'll have to excuse me."

"Where are you going?" Lucas called after him.

"To take back my name," Jesse said.

Oh, shit . . .

The door slamming shut startled me even more than his words, at least until they began to sink in deeper. Lucas shifted uneasily, undoubtedly knowing what I had also figured out: Jesse wrote that email Lucas had read last night.

"Don't worry, I'm sure he'll be okay," I said, trying to comfort him.

Lucas shook his head. "I feel like something bad's about to happen, and I don't know how to stop it," he whispered.

"I don't, either."

JAMES

"I'M SORRY I'VE BEEN SUCH AN IDIOT." IT WAS A PLEA more than it was an apology, but all the same, Heather seemed receptive.

"It's okay, James," she said, even though I knew it wasn't.

"I was reading *Hamlet* with Will last night," I continued, "and he was able to help me with some of the Old English."

Heather's eyebrows raised as if she'd never met me before. "Will's into Shakespeare?" Now that she said it out loud, I realized how strange it really did sound.

I shrugged, but groaned in pain from where Dad's blow had landed on me. "Who'da thought, right?"

Opening the door for her to show proper respect, even knowing I'd never get her back, was a pleasure. It was nice to breathe a sigh of relief, regardless of expectation. A small moment of happiness was something I didn't realize I desperately needed until I had it.

As I walked into class, I stopped cold. For some

reason, it felt like the weather changed, which was impossible because we were indoors. The clack of a boot echoed from the other side of the hallway, and I didn't like the sound of it at all. It was ominous as fuck.

My eyes darted down the other way, and some small figure crept toward me, a silhouette in the daytime. "It's you," was all I could muster when I saw it was that poor kid, the one I helped Will hurt.

The door shut behind me and nearly startled me half to death. We were alone in the hallway, and I'd never been so scared in all my life. What had Will done to this kid?

There was another bandage on his right wrist, and he shook uncontrollably. His eyes seemed empty, lost in the sea of black that was his outfit, and it was like he'd already given up.

Don't do anything stupid, kid. Worth a shot to try to fix open wounds, right?

Damn, poor choice of words . . .

"Look," I began, "I'm really sorry about the other day . . ." I tried to be as sincere as possible, hoping he'd see it in my smile.

"I'm sure you are," he muttered coldly. Was he shaking, or was I? Shit . . .

"I am," I insisted. "It took seeing things a different way, but I am. Someone opened my eyes." Maybe the Voice could open his eyes too. That was how I learned to have hope again.

"That's a shame," the kid answered, "they'll be closed again very soon." Then he pulled a handgun from his pocket and pointed it at me.

Holy fuck!

I threw my hands up immediately, my dad's training igniting instincts I didn't even know I had. "What the fuck are you doing?!" I cried out, hoping to shake him from this trance.

"Making you pay," he responded, the gun quaking in his hands. "Making all of you pay for what you've done to me."

"Put the gun down!" I demanded out of pure fear. "This is real life!"

Tears started streaming down his face, and I experienced a brief moment of hope, thinking I'd at least reached him. Eyeliner made dark rivers over his cheeks, making him look like the damn Crow.

Fuck, Will, why did you have to be such an asshole?

"I'm not a man!" he screamed. "I'm a fucking fag, according to you!" He pulled his hood down, and I suddenly recognized him. It wasn't a guy, it was Jessica! Or what used to be Jessica . . . She'd cut her hair, and I guess restrained her chest, but that was definitely Jessica. When did she start being a guy? Or trying to look like one? And how the fuck did it come to this?

The door opened behind me, and I panicked. Turning around to stop whoever it was, I heard Heather's voice yelling, "James!" in terror. A loud bang followed, and then everything vanished.

JESSE

DID I MISS?
They'd kill me if I missed.

VERONICA

WHAT THE FUCK WAS THAT?

LUCAS

"JESSE . . . NO . . ."

MARK

WHAT'S GOING ON OUT THERE?

JAMES

I EXPECTED THE PAIN TO HIT ANY SECOND. ONE EYE scrunched, I peeked to look down at my chest, and mercifully saw nothing there. He'd missed, thank god.

Jesse, holding his ears from the reverb, dropped to the floor until he noticed I was looking.

Then what sounded like a tiny drop of rain hitting the floor barely caught my attention. I glanced down. Blood. I followed it up to Heather as another drop of blood splattered on the ground.

Grasping her stomach, she looked down as one hand moved away to reveal a growing bloodstain on her sweater.

"Shit," she whispered before slumping in the vestibule in front of the classroom.

Screams started ringing out from everywhere, but all I had on my mind was Heather. I crashed to my knees in front of her and cradled her head in my arms. She was quickly falling into unconsciousness.

"No, no, no!" I pleaded, trying to keep her awake.

Jessica, goddammit! He . . . she? Whoever they were

had hurt Heather, the nicest person I'd ever met in my life. Glaring at him, even in his state, I couldn't help but yell, "She had nothing to do with this!" Every fiber of my being shook.

Not her. Not Heather. Shoot me again and help her, you fucking asshole! Not Heather!

Doors sprung open everywhere as more screams and cries flooded the hallway. The emergency alarm sounded and students began tripping over each other, trying to get to the exit.

For a second, I thought I saw Will running toward the scene. Couldn't have been . . .

LUCAS

I HADN'T MADE IT IN TIME. SOMEONE WAS HURT, AND I saw a bloodstain on the floor. As I approached, I realized Heather had been shot. James was tending to her, but of all people beginning to try to talk Jesse down . . . Will?

"Just put the gun down," he pleaded with Jesse.

"You have no idea how much trouble I'm in," Jesse sobbed, gnashing his teeth.

"I do, more than you know," Will, remaining calm, surprisingly agreed. Who was this guy, and what he done with the Will who'd tormented this very kid?

Jesse's breathing became erratic, and the gun was back up, pointing at Will. "You don't know a goddamn thing!" Jesse exclaimed, taking one step closer. I slid toward him from the other side as quietly as I could.

"What's my name?" Jesse demanded.

Will stared. "What?"

I was now in Jesse's field of vision, and I held up my hand toward him. A lot of good that would do with a gun, but it was all I could think of. "Please, don't do this."

Jesse's gaze didn't move from Will. "I have to, before he hurts anyone else." After a beat, he yelled even louder, "What's my name, Will?"

"I don't . . ." Will began.

"Say my fucking name!" Jesse shook the nearby door as he lost it. "You took the time to ruin every single day I had in this school! You found me every day, and you don't even realize you already knew me. You tried to fuck me, you ignorant son of a bitch!"

"What are you talking about?"

"She used to be Jessica," James piped up, still holding Heather in the corner.

"Jessica?" Will's glare of recognition became deadly serious. "What happened to you?"

"I became who I really was," Jesse answered, "who I've always been. But instead of recognizing that, you just thought I was some feminine boy that you could torment. You didn't see the tears in my eyes, the scars on my wrists, or the effects all your shitty actions had. You only laughed and walked away, like you did when I refused your advances."

Jesse took one step closer, more adamant than ever. This was gonna get ugly, one way or another. "You took my name away!" he followed up at the top of his lungs. "Tell me what it was, Will! Tell us what you did! Say my fucking name!"

Will's shoulders slumped, defeated. "I'm sorry, Jessica."

"My name is fucking Jesse, goddammit!"

"We hazed you because you were there, same as what happened to me when I was a freshman."

"I'm not a freshman! I'm a goddamn senior like you!"

"It was never personal," Will replied. "And I'm sorry for hurting you, you know . . . back then."

"I suppose that was never personal, either?"

"No, that was," Will confessed. "But I'm sorry. I promise you, the hazing you went through this year, we didn't know. Like I said, it wasn't personal at all."

Jesse pulled back the hammer on his gun. "It was personal to me."

I needed to do something, now. I stepped closer to him, not enough to scare him away, but enough that he could easily hear me. "This isn't what the Voice meant by taking back your name, Jesse."

Jesse turned his head toward me in a moment of recognition. "What?"

Seizing the moment, Will charged Jesse and grabbed the gun. Jesse kept his grip, doing his best to fight off the larger Will. Unwilling to let Will hurt him any more than he already had, I wrestled Jesse away from him to the ground, those old mat instincts from junior high returning to me at a very convenient moment. Locking him in a full nelson, I kept him there until he stopped fighting back.

I realized he was being forced to look at James and Heather in the corner. Heather was passed out now.

JESSE

NO! I NEVER MEANT TO HURT HER! HOW DID THIS happen?!

"I'm so sorry," I managed to say before my tears completely overtook me.

"It's okay," that comforting voice that had stood up for me replied in earnest. "I'm right here with you."

Don't worry, I thought to myself. *I won't tell them who you really are. They'll come after you next.*

JAMES

WILL PICKED UP THE GUN AND UNLOADED IT SLOWLY, letting each remaining bullet drop to the floor one by one.

He then turned, his eyes connecting with mine in a moment of understanding before turning down the hallway. "We need some help down here!"

Someone handed me a t-shirt and I pressed it to the wound. Shock had set in, and I was feeling nothing but terror for my former love.

My eyes also caught a moment where Lucas and Will nodded at each other.

I'll be damned . . . never thought I'd see the day.

Why did it have to take this to get us to stop being shitty to each other for two fucking minutes?

VERONICA

"HEATHER!"

PRINCIPAL SAWYER

OH, JESUS, NO...

LUCAS

VERONICA DID HER BEST TO BRING PRINCIPAL SAWYER to the scene, but she dropped to the floor when she saw Heather. Veronica darted over to her and helped James comfort her. Her eyes made contact with mine, and I didn't know what to do. Whatever I chose might mess things up even more than I already had.

This was all my fault.

All this blood, this chaos, this pain . . . all of it was my fault.

Police sirens sounded in the difference, rapidly getting closer.

"Finally," was all I could say. What else was there?

JAMES

"No, no, no!"

Principal Sawyer and the EMTs took Heather away to the ambulance as quickly as possible. "She's alive," one of them confirmed, "but we have to get her to the hospital right away. She has internal bleeding."

I pushed my way through one of them, noticing how blood-soaked my clothes were, yet hardly caring. I gripped Heather's hand. The fact that we were no longer together was irrelevant. I only hoped Liz hadn't seen this.

"Are you family?" one of them asked.

"No, but I'm not leaving her."

"Family only, sir," he ordered. "Please step away."

"Let him go," pleaded Principal Sawyer for my sake.

"I'm sorry," the EMT replied.

The door closed, and they banged on it twice. The sirens penetrated my ear drums, and I dropped to my knees in absolute disbelief. For one solitary second in time, it felt like Principal Sawyer and I were watching the end of a really bad movie.

Reporters and photographers crowded the front door of the school. I did my best to keep my cool, avoiding talking to anyone, especially with who my dad was.

Then they brought him out. Him. The one who did it. The one who shot Heather, who never hurt anyone.

I dove at him as hard as I could, but the throng of police officers held me back, restraining me until they got him into the car. I'd never felt so helpless in my entire life.

A huge cheer arose from the crowd surrounding me. Who on earth could cheer at such a time?

LUCAS

FOR THE FIRST TIME IN ... WELL, EVER ... WILL AND I emerged from somewhere at the same time. A wave of yelling crested the second we exited, nearly pushing us back. This wasn't good. I couldn't be here. Too many people. This was freaky. My breathing quickened ... I knew what was happening.

As I tried to slip out the back of the crowd, a reporter shoved his microphone in my face. "Can you tell us what happened?" he demanded.

Desperately, I looked toward the guy who was used to the media interrogation. Unfortunately, members of the press were already milking that for all he was worth.

I turned back toward the impatient guy. "Worry about Heather right now," I replied. "That's what's important."

"How does it feel to be a hero, son?" another inquired.

I motioned toward the football star. "Will is the real hero," I deferred. "You should be talking to him."

"How do you feel about the Voice?" a different interrogator questioned. I stopped cold, trying not to lose my cool. "Do you think he caused this?"

"Excuse me?" I responded incredulously.

"Columbus Evening News has discovered that the anonymous podcaster known only as the Voice may have instigated these events by encouraging the accused to take action," he ranted as if the cameras were live, which they probably were.

"Yeah, do you know who he is?" the second one added.

"Have you ever listened to the Voice?"

My face was flushing. I needed to get away from these people before I had a panic attack and gave myself away.

"The Voice had nothing to do with this!" I exclaimed, and then bull rushed my way through the crowd. I wasn't having any of it. The focus didn't need to be on me . . . or the other me . . . in any way.

Before I could escape the mob, Dad marched toward the front of the school, Don following close behind.

Great . . .

Dad, in full uniform, and Don acting like he was in fucking Iraq or something, the way he was scoping the place out. *They already have the shooter in custody, ya douche.*

"Mr. Commissioner!" the Action Live Now idiot called out. "Can you tell us what's going on? Are there any charges being filed?"

My dad stepped forward while Don remained at attention. Secret Service now? This guy was delusional.

"This event took place because the principal dismissed the head of security," Dad said as he motioned toward Don. "Mr. Donald Kasich here."

Wait, that was James' dad? You had to be kidding me. Don stepped up to receive the applause that was likely only emanating from his own head.

"Because of there being nobody to enforce the zero-tolerance security measures implemented over the past year," Dad continued, "a gun was brought into school by a kid who had no history of bad behavior. It is believed that he may have been encouraged by a third party."

The media screamed various things about the Voice, and I covered my ears. Everything was getting too loud.

"It may have been the Voice," Dad conceded, "but we aren't sure of anything yet. Nobody seems to know anything about this anonymous instigator, but I swear to you, that will change. I needed someone familiar with his work, so therefore . . ."

Fuck . . .

"I have not only reinstated Mr. Kasich here," Dad said, proudly placing his hand on the shoulder of the scum of the earth, "but I have given him the utmost authority to help the police do whatever is necessary to find the Voice and bring him in for questioning."

Don smiled like the sick fuck he was.

"If he encouraged the young man to, at the very least, attempt a murder on a fellow student," Dad surmised, "then he must be brought to justice, just as the young man who committed this action was. That is all, thank you."

I covered my ears as the press lobbed more questions at my father. Nobody was going to notice me here, so I dropped to the ground and buried myself near the steps until they lost interest. At some point, I'm pretty sure I began breathing again.

There was no way I could go on again. No. Fucking. Way.

The third reporter greased up his hair like he was in the 50s and turned toward the camera like he was born to report the bad news. "This is Joe Manning, Columbus Area News . . ."

MARTHA

"ANOTHER HORRIFYING SCHOOL SHOOTING HAS TAKEN place in America," Joe Manning from the evening news explained, "and today, it is in our own backyard. One student has been hospitalized, the alleged shooter is being held, and still out there . . . somewhere . . . is the anonymous agitator only known as 'the Voice.'"

I glanced at my son. "Do you know who this guy is?"

Lucas shook his head. Poor kid was probably a mess from everything that happened today. I shouldn't have pushed.

"No one has yet stepped forward to be questioned, as it is confirmed that the alleged shooter wrote this Voice an email and that he instructed the student to, quote, 'take back his name.' The alleged shooter has also confirmed as such, and says he was out to take back his own name from those who disgraced it. This is Columbus Area News, I'm Joe Manning."

Could that guy be any more smug?

"Lucas, please eat something," I implored my son.

He was a wreck, and I imagined another one of his anxiety attacks had plagued his appetite. He stared down at his plate without moving, so I tried to help as best I could. "Do you know who this guy is? Maybe there's something you can tell your father to help them find him?"

"The Voice didn't tell him to go shoot somebody, Mom," he barely whispered back at me.

"I know you listen to that show, Lucas," I started. Lucas stood up, making his chair screech on the floor. "But please!" I shouted after him. "If you know anything about him, you must tell your father!"

The pounding up the steps ceased, and I desperately tried one last time. "Lucas!"

He slammed the door. No luck tonight.

Marissa Alexa McCool

VERONICA

I DIDN'T KNOW WHY I WAS OUT ON THE STREETS tonight. Perhaps it was because my mother was desperate for one of those bonding conversations at the worst possible time. But maybe, just maybe, it was because I was hoping Tall, Dark, and Handsome would be like me—nomadic and restless. He was so strong for everyone else that I couldn't help feeling that someone needed to be strong for him.

Somehow, that instinct must've been matched.

There he was, strolling about the empty Columbus streets as if we hadn't seen one of our classmates getting shot. His own planet, drifting away toward a different reality, a way to cope with the world that seemed too impossible to be the one on which we were destined to stay.

Approaching as carefully as I could, I matched his stride before making my presence known. I asked the question that had to be the most idiotic thing I've ever asked "How are you holding up?"

Stupid Veronica, what kind of question is that on a

145

day like this?!

"I don't know," he stammered barely above a whisper. "I can't believe this is real."

"I know." What else could I say?

We walked in icy silence, both of us clearly trained to hide our emotions rather than purge them through any kind of catharsis. I opted for changing the subject.

"Heather's in critical condition," I informed him. He may have saved her life, so he deserved to know.

He didn't respond, so I knew he was taking it hard. "It wasn't your fault," I offered.

"Wasn't it?" he challenged.

I couldn't take it anymore. I grabbed both his shoulders and looked him dead in the eye. "No, it wasn't!"

I knew what I had to do. It was going to be harder to get through to him than I thought, so perhaps he needed evidence, persuasion, or a firm slap in the damn face. For someone so intelligent and articulate, he sure could be fucking frustrating too.

"I think you should come with me," I told him. "You need to see something."

LUCAS

WHAT THE HELL WERE WE DOING AT THE FOOTBALL field? Why was this girl taking me back to school? This was the last place in the world I wanted to be, save for maybe my parents' living room.

All at once, the activity on the athletic area came into view like the opening of a movie. Cars, students, candles, but most of all, signs. A lot of them referencing the word *Nameless*. "I am Nameless." Then, that gothic punk-looking guy who got punched by Don stood above them all with a giant one: "We Are All Nameless."

"What's Nameless?" I wondered out loud.

"You are," she responded without looking back at me.

"Wait," I stuttered, the realization hitting me. "What?"

She turned toward me, a knowing but stern expression decorating her face. "Why don't you look at what this has turned into?"

"I don't understand."

This girl was somewhere in between wanting to

kiss me and kill me, and I wasn't sure which was the closer preference at this moment in time. She stepped toward the field and turned to me, the lights flickering over her indignant glance.

"Yes," she began, "that fucked-up security guard and the police commissioner think you might have had something to do with it, but look at all those kids out there who have heard your voice and are on your side."

"They don't even know who I am," I argued. "They called me Nameless."

"They're showing solidarity," she gritted. "You're an anonymous voice, but you're the one we need. It's only going to get worse—surely you know that better than anyone else. You told Jesse to take back his name, and he took it way too far, but now all of us are like that. We all have a name we need to take back, and until we do ... until the corruption of these motherfuckers is exposed ... we are all Nameless."

I stepped in front of her and observed a little more closely this time. A framed picture of Heather held the vigil together, and standing nearby, of all people, was Will.

"Will is here?" I asked, noticing that neither he, nor anyone else, wore their trademark letter jackets.

"Everyone is here," she confirmed. "You need to go on tonight, for them."

So that's what this was about. "Won't they be able to find out where I am?"

"Already got it covered," she replied without missing a beat.

"What the hell does that mean?"

"Don't worry about it. Just get on the air. For them,

and for everyone else out there who stands behind you. Your words have impacted everyone who has ever heard them. This school has needed Nameless for so long, and now all of them need to hear you. The media aren't going to comfort them. The police aren't going to comfort them. They need you."

She motioned toward my house in the distance. "Go. I'll be here."

JOE MANNING

THIS WAS PERFECT. WHAT MORE COULD A SMALL-TOWN reporter ask for? Kids getting shot, gender questions, an anonymous podcaster riling everyone up . . . this was my ticket to the big-time. No more Columbus, no more cats stuck in trees, but the Nightly News with Joe Manning. *Good evening, everyone. Good evening . . . to you. And you.*

"We'll be listening for the Nameless Voice tonight, but we hope he does the right thing and turns himself in," the police chief said. "If he has nothing to hide, that shouldn't be any problem."

His wife stood in the background looking like someone just kicked a cat. I'd fuck her. Hell, I might even call her afterward.

Then that nutcase barged his own way on screen and lit up like a 9/11 truther: "Nameless, I'm coming for you. Believe that!"

This kept getting better. I barely had to editorialize anything—these whack jobs did it for me.

"Emotions are running high as the students wait to

hear from their anonymous voice," I said, delivering my lines as smoothly as Cronkite in his prime. "What will he have to say about the poor young girl hospitalized because of what he said?"

Bam, Joe. You are killing this. Oops, should I say that when someone might die? Fuck it, take it home, you handsome devil.

"This is Joe Manning, Columbus Evening News," I concluded with a wink for all the network stars surely lining up to sign this guy fresh out of the disaster zone.

I glanced out at these idiot kids, gathered on the football field to listen to a recording of a radio show, or whatever a podcast was. Dumbasses, all of them. Only a paycheck to me.

A loud burst of feedback made me jump. The kids erupted in cheers like Paul McCartney had walked out to a crowd of young girls in the 60s. Man, all these sheltered fools needed to get out of Columbus. At least after this story had run its course.

DON

THERE HE WAS. I KNEW HE WOULDN'T DISAPPOINT. HE might have been a punk, but he was nothing if not consistent and punctual. A few police sirens cried out, and I heard them echo into the night.

"Are we going to find him?" I eagerly inquired over the police chief's shoulder.

He brushed me back as if he hadn't hired me to be his right hand man. Maybe he preferred being approached on the left or something. Cops were weird.

"You may have your job back," he responded, "but don't forget who I am. We go after him when *I* say so, not you."

Great, he was just as inane as the principal. I was gonna have to take matters into my own hands, but only at the right time.

"I heard you've been looking for me," a voice taunted over the speakers on the field. It was him. Why couldn't we trace this signal and take him down now? What more proof did these people need that he was a dangerous instigator that needed to be apprehended?

"You want to know who I am," he said, "what I'm doing, where I am, and how I single-handedly caused the tearing of the very fabric of this school's society. Who knows, maybe I caused the recession too. Well, I only have one thing to say to you . . ."

I'm sorry? I'm an asshole? I'm dropping out? I insist you take me straight to jail where I belong? Come on, kid, stop wasting my time.

"I. Am. Nameless!" he proclaimed.

"Disgusting," I couldn't help but mutter out loud, hoping Lionel heard me.

"Should we start?" one of Lionel's officers asked him.

He held up his hand in a futile effort to abate the tension, no doubt. "Give it a few minutes."

That was wise. At least we'd be able to shove this kid's words back in his fucking face after he taunted us in front of the whole school. Anonymous coward. We'd give him a name.

Coward. Coward will be your name. Shove Nameless up your ass, unless you like that sort of thing.

LIZ

BRIAN WRAPPED HIS ARMS GENTLY AROUND ME, BUT MY eyes couldn't drift from the picture of Heather. She'd never done anything wrong. Why? Why would someone do this to my girl? Why, once I was finally happy, did some kid have to take that away from me?

The crowd around us fell silent, quite like the vigil for my girlfriend had before the show started. "We're here for you, man," Brian said, even though the Voice obviously couldn't hear him.

"Say what you gotta say," I pointlessly added.

"I'm sorry, Heather," the Voice began. Dammit. My eyes were getting hot. It wasn't his fault, but I couldn't mistake the burning in my chest for anything but the thirst for revenge.

But I knew I couldn't blame the Voice any more than I could blame Sean or Brian. We were only trying to get through the day with as little pain as possible.

That was what most of these adults supervising us and poking into our daily lives didn't understand. We weren't hiding any secrets. We weren't planning

154

anything. We just wanted to make it through the day without getting shot. Was that so much to ask? And did they have to treat us all like criminals in the process? Even the justice enforcers needed justice and enforcement.

"Regardless of who caused it and why it happened," the Voice continued, "I am so sorry this happened to you. I never said 'don't hurt anyone else.' I'm sorry, Heather. I'm sorry, Liz. I'm sorry, James. I'm sorry, everyone listening. This isn't what I wanted to happen."

My arms clasped onto the next person standing near me, as I could tell Brian wasn't exactly the affectionate type.

Wait, I knew these arms.

"It's gonna be okay," Sean whispered in my ear. "I know you felt something for her."

"Everything," was all I mustered between the tears now streaming down my face.

Brian stared directly at the speakers, as if he expected the Voice to turn into a corporeal person before our very eyes. I wasn't sure if that would help or not at this point, but regardless, we were with him. He was the only one not speculating and using us for media attention or corruption.

Heather didn't deserve this.

Please, god, don't take her. She's the love of my life.

PRINCIPAL SAWYER

I TUNED MY HEADSET RADIO, EVEN THOUGH I COULD hear the Voice just fine from the parking lot. If it meant not having to deal with Don's "I told you so" schtick one more time, it was worth it to at least appear distracted.

"...and those who are looking for me, they only cite me as a reason for the tragedy that happened today. They're not willing to look at the system, or the people in it, or those fucking crazy security guys who hit their own kids."

This kid was playing with fire. A part of me had to admire his courage and assertiveness, but this was going to get out of control fast, and I had to do something.

Don was already in a rage. No huge surprise there. It was time to do what was necessary, as much as it hurt, and as much as it pained me to try to quiet a voice that our school probably needed more than ever.

"That's it," Don yelled, "I'm finding this son of a bitch!" He started storming around the parking lot.

"Does anyone have a place I can trace this source? Maybe we can find out where he's broadcasting from!"

He'd seen too many movies, but if it kept him occupied and not hitting people, it was worth it to at least throw a Hail Mary and see what happened.

"Don, you may use the office to trace the IP," I consented, almost sure I knew what those words meant. "I want this guy found immediately," I added to cover my regret and utter distaste for the man.

LUCAS

YOU'RE IN DEEP SHIT NOW, LUCAS. A PRETTY GIRL TELLS you what to do, and you go on the air, even when your dad is police chief and definitely on the prowl, not to mention Don.

I dreamed of the day where I could punch that man like he'd hit his own son, but I'd at least do it to his face.

"If you want to ignore every circumstance that finally led to someone letting loose and instead blame me," I said breezily, "that's fine. Come after me. I can handle it."

Who was I, fucking Batman? This was insane, and I knew I was getting in way deeper than I could handle, but it didn't matter anymore. Something spoke through me that I never realized was there.

"What Jesse did was wrong," I admitted, though I still felt awful for the kid and what he went through. It didn't excuse shooting someone, but the nerve of these phonies to act like it had no root cause was even worse. "I don't approve of how he handled his situation."

As if that made any fucking difference at this point.

Now it was time for the part I was going to get nailed for.

No backing down, Lucas. This is what you started this show for. You wouldn't be legitimate if you didn't speak up when it was needed the most.

"But how can you be surprised that a kid lashed out?" Nothing was stopping me now. "How can you sit there with blinders on, ignoring what the kid of zero-tolerance security you've implemented has done? When you have kids suspended for standing up for themselves, giving them equal punishment as those who walk the halls, making the most vulnerable among us afraid to go to school every day—what message does that send?"

It was true. If I had punched James or Will back, I would've gotten suspended too, because that's the world we lived in. Equal punishment: One for bullies, and one for those who weren't going to take it anymore. I was now the latter, and it was going to be far worse than suspension. I didn't care anymore. Fuck them. Fuck anyone who supported this shit.

"Your selective enforcement of the rules, giving others privilege while trying to run others considered undesirable out of school, is fucking shameful, and I'm not going to apologize for speaking out about it!"

DOCTOR

I STARED THROUGH THE GLASS WINDOW AT THE POOR girl whose wound I'd sewn up. Poor kid, she was so beautiful. Who could shoot someone like this? Fucking kids. I needed a cigarette.

VERONICA

STANDING APART FROM THE CROWD TO ENSURE NOBODY was around me, I stared at the giant speakers and where Heather's picture sat. Nothing but justice was going to resolve this, and nobody was willing to say it but him: the Voice. Nameless.

"An innocent girl is in the hospital," he reminded us all, "because too many people were covering their eyes and plugging their ears, not seeing the blatantly clear signs that someone needed help. Probably a lot more do, but this got instigated at the right time against the wrong person. Probably one of the kids the fucking head of security was trying to kick out of school for tainting his 1950s image of what a student should be."

There was the Nameless I was falling in love with. There was the voice that haunted my dreams and decorated my fantasies.

"This dickhead goes out of his way to find those he doesn't approve of and ruin their records forever by placing phony disciplinary marks all over them," Lucas hissed. Maybe it wasn't exactly like that, but it sure as hell felt that way. "Maybe because they're societal outliers, or freaks, or fags, or goths, or emo kids, or any of the other people who walked these fucking hallowed halls every single day. Those ones—the ones who don't throw a ball or lift a pom-pom, who don't feel like they belong anywhere—I'm one of them, and we're all fucking sick of it!"

MARK

THIS HAD ALL GOTTEN WAY TOO HEAVY. I WAS NOW dealing with police scanners and diverting the signal as much as I could, but there was only so much I could do from this computer. I was dealing with professionals now.

Firewall blocked! appeared in blue. I relaxed for a second so I could hear what he was saying.

"They don't fear me because they think I abetted Jesse," he exclaimed. *Of course not, Nameless. None of us do.* "They fear me because I'm telling you not to take it anymore. Because no change can come from everyone remaining in the status quo. So long as I'm an outlier, so long as nobody riles anyone up or bucks the system, the status quo will remain the same, and bullies will be excused, validated, and gain confidence."

A long moment of silence followed, but then I heard beeps that indicated my job was far from done. "Kill it, Nameless," I encouraged him as I went back to work.

"This stops now," he declared.

Preach it!

"Thanks for the IP address," I typed onto the screen that I knew whoever was trying to find Nameless would see. What's a cyber-crime if you can't also troll a little bit?

I relaxed, then shot straight up when I heard the door opening.

For Christ's sake, Dad, knock once in a while!

"Are you playing a game again?" he asked.

"Nope, just running a little tech support," I said, a partial truth. Not like he would read between the lines.

"Well, as long as you aren't listening to that radio guy," Dad said as he closed the door behind him.

Yeah, wouldn't that be a shame?

DON

I BURST THROUGH THE COMPUTER LAB DOOR, READY TO apprehend this motherfucker once and for all. How could he be so foolish as to broadcast from here?

"All of you out there," the criminal proclaimed, "stand up! Rise up! You don't have to take this anymore!"

Yes, you do, Nameless Coward.

"Don't fucking shoot anyone! But don't let them take your names away!"

I'm going to, starting with yours, Coward. I ran toward the back corner where I assumed he was hiding. One of the computers was on.

"Thanks for the IP address," the screen read.

"Goddammit!" I screamed. "He hacked through the school's system! Shut it down!"

BRIAN

"BURN IT," I MUTTERED, "BURN IT TO THE GROUND."

The wave started behind me, and shit was getting real. Might as well go with it. These assholes needed a wake-up call.

The whine of a megaphone sounded from the fucking police chief, as if the apologetics he offered earlier were going to calm down this bunch. His shaky voice rang out across the stadium.

"Students, disperse from this location immediately!"

"No!" I heard a hundred students cry in defiance of his orders. A rhythmic chant started, and I couldn't help but smile while looking for the dead-wooded prick head of security. This moment of victory would be nice to witness with him there.

The riot-geared officers started forming in the parking lot. Oh, shit, they weren't fucking around. Time to move this to public property.

I stood up on the pickup truck holding the speakers and raised my fist. Several hundred raised back in unison, and I pointed toward the street leading to the city.

"I am Nameless!" I proclaimed, hoping they'd get that I was calling for unity and not confessing to being someone who was also somehow broadcasting live.

"I am Nameless!" the crowd echoed in return, and just like that, we were marching toward the city street before any of those riot pigs could get organized. The other cops were waiting for one of us to do something stupid as they stood by with their hands on their weapons.

No need to get squirrely, officers. Only the First Amendment being used on our side, for a change.

We marched and chanted into the night. For once in our lives, we felt truly free.

MISS HUNTER

What was I even doing here? What was going to happen to these kids? What could I teach them that was going to help them out of this situation?

I was just about to turn off the bedroom light when I heard a knock at the door. Who on earth could that be at this hour?

I grabbed some mace, just in case. A young lady in a strange town can never be too careful. Peering through the crack in the door, I asked, "Who is it?"

"Mark, your student?"

Mark? The somewhat-nerdy one who insisted on following the syllabus? Oh, he wasn't going to hurt anyone.

I unchained the door, opened it up, and saw him there; face red, cheeks tear-stained, and a stack of papers in his hand.

"What can I do for you, Mark?" I tried to sound as nonchalant as possible, but no one could reasonably expect that today. Not today.

"I need you to see these. You're the only one I can

trust."

"What are they?"

"You'll find out," he said. "Don't tell anyone who gave them to you."

"But Mark . . ." I tried to protest, but he was already running away, terrified, into the night.

The stack of papers trembled in my hands as I hoped it wasn't a warning of worse things to come. The last thing anyone needed here was more bloodshed.

Glancing down at the top one, I felt the air rush out of my lungs, and I desperately searched for a couch to crash on. I missed, and the papers flew everywhere. Seeing the scattered pages made me realize something—every one was like that first one.

"You're not a boy and you never will be, dyke," it read.

"You ain't got a dick, but I got one for you. I'll shove it up your ass if you wanna feel like a faggot."

"Fuck you, bitch, I'm gonna call you what's on your birth certificate."

"I better not catch you wearing guy clothes around the hall. Bad things happen. Just saying."

Each one was as difficult to read as the next, and I couldn't help but let the tears fall on the pages. Did it excuse what he did? No. But desperate actions can at least have some context, can't they?

"You're Jessica, not Jesse. Why can't you just call yourself a lesbian?"

"Die, cunt."

"If you wanna be a boy so bad, go a few rounds with me. I'll show you how tough you are. Get back in the kitchen, bitch."

Every single page was a hate message that had ended up in his email, Facebook, Myspace . . . anywhere this poor kid tried to find acceptance, he was rejected and threatened every step of the way.

All except for one.

And he's the one they're blaming for everything.

Something had to be done about this. Immediately.

LUCAS

MY PHONE BUZZED IN MY POCKET ON THE WAY TO school. It was a picture of today's headline in the *Columbus Ledger*. Security Measures to Increase After Tragedy at Columbus.

Great. Just fucking great.

I checked everywhere around me to make sure I wasn't being followed and tried to tunnel-vision it the whole way to school.

Walking around a corner, I felt someone grasp my hand and I panicked. Already high-strung and paranoid, I was ready to run until I saw it was Veronica, holding my hand in comfort. I could live with that, but for fuck's sake, I wished she hadn't snuck up on me. My anxiety was through the roof as it was!

She squeezed my hand, probably to prompt me to look at her, and when I did, my cheeks flushed. I couldn't help it—she was really freaking pretty. How had I not noticed that, or at least taken the time to acknowledge it?

Despite everything going on, my journey to school

became more relaxed. Our little pairing took what was going on in the world out of my mind for a few seconds, and allowed me some solitude in knowing that one thing in one place was at least okay. Somewhat okay.

Turning the last corner toward Columbus High, we nearly ran smack into a brick wall of students waiting to get inside.

"It's like Black Friday out here," observed Veronica. "What's going on?"

"Increased security," I reported.

Her face revealed that she wasn't aware of this. "Increased security? How much more can they increase it?"

"Don't ask that," I warned, fearing the worst.

Two people brushed into us, and I felt the tension in my stomach tighten. Too much. Everything was getting too loud, and it was too crowded.

"Sorry about that," the girl apologized. I recognized her, but I couldn't place it. Or at least not at the moment, because I was losing it. And myself.

"It's almost like a mosh-pit in here," a guy added. Great, someone was gonna throw a punch. I didn't know if I was ready to defend myself. Or should I even have had to? What were the security guards packing? Who knew what Dad allowed them this time?

"Hey Veronica!" I heard another familiar voice shout. James. Son of a bitch, he was coming for me again after what happened. My breathing was getting heavier, and I didn't know what to do. I needed out. I needed to get away.

"Can you believe this?" he asked once he got near

us.

"Oh look, 1984 already," Veronica mused. I couldn't help but chuckle at that remark. Thought Crime was a likely possibility with Don's new initiative.

"It'll take them forever to move on from what happened," another voice continued. Will. The walls were closing in, and I was surrounded by potential enemies. I tried to speak, but couldn't. Fuck. Get me out of here! "Though some of us have a knack for doing that quicker than others," he finished, staring intently at Veronica, who was still holding my hand.

Fuck, fuck, fuck, a fight was coming and I didn't need it. I didn't need any of this! It was a mistake going on the air last night. All of this was a mistake. I should've never said anything.

"We're all gonna be late if you don't let us in!" James yelled, oblivious to anything going on while Veronica's ex stared daggers into both of us.

"Have you heard anything about Heather?" the guy who had bumped into me asked, then turned to me "I'm Sean, by the way."

"Liz," the girl added, tears still in her eyes. This must've been Heather's girlfriend.

Someone tapped on James' shoulder, and he turned away from me to see who it was. "She's still in critical condition," Mark told him, "but she's alive."

Mark? How did Mark know any of these people?

"So you've seen her?" James inquired.

"No," Mark admitted, "last night I was running interference for Nameless, and . . ."

The crowd seemed to fall silent around us. Everyone stared at Mark, who had revealed a connection to . . . well, me.

"You know Nameless?" Will asked.

"Who is he?" Sean followed up.

"Do you have any idea?" Liz added.

"How did you get to be working for him?" James asked.

Mark threw up his hands, overwhelmed. "Guys, guys!" he pleaded. "He contacted me anonymously a while ago. I rerouted his IP address through the school itself, but since they shut the school's Internet down, I can't do it anymore."

I took note of that, realizing any time I went on from here on out wouldn't be protected.

"I set up his school email address," James confessed. The group around us now seemed more surprised. "I used my dad's security clearance to do it."

"No, that was me," Mark countered.

James, taken aback, retreated a step and stared in admiration, or to be threatening, I wasn't sure. "I didn't realize we had a connection," James finally replied.

"You never asked," replied Mark. "You were more content with just giving me shit every day."

"Well," James meekly tried to respond, but his shoulders slumped in defeat. "It took someone pointing it out to show me the error of my ways. Unfortunately, Jesse didn't let me get there. I wish he could've heard me. Heather wouldn't be where she is right now if he had."

James' face was filled with regret and sorrow. I couldn't imagine what mine looked like, but I tried to remain invisible, something I was really good at in this conversation.

To everyone's utter amazement, Mark reached out and hugged James, even though he had to reach up to do it. "I heard you," he said.

Wow, this was really happening.

Before James could say anything, Sergeant Dickhead appeared at the top of the main stairwell with his trusty megaphone. Two security officers held Brian beside him. Brian tried to resist, but they overpowered him into submission.

"Attention, all students!" Don declared. "There are additional security measures through which all students must pass. Due to the events that have taken place recently, if you are unwilling to go through security, you will be sent home!"

Don glanced over at Brian, a sick grin spreading across his face. Fuck, now we were all being targeted. They'd given the jester the keys to the kingdom.

"And if you are caught, in any capacity, having a relationship with—or knowing the identity of—anyone with a connection to Nameless, you will be reprimanded. If you do not give us his identity, you will be suspended."

A collective groan resounded throughout the mass of students.

"This school sucks!" Veronica declared.

"Bullshit!" Sean spat.

Don motioned for the officers to take Brian away. "You can't do this!" Brian shouted, sounding vulnerable for the first time since I'd noticed his presence in school.

"Meet our first victim," Don continued, almost boastful. "The organizer of last night's riot, and the reason why these security measures will continue until Nameless is found and questioned. You can all keep up with the charade if you want, but you will face the consequences."

"I have rights, you rent-a-cop fuckwit!" Brian screamed in pure terror.

"I won't be hearing that anymore!" Don responded defiantly. He turned toward all of us. "Anyone interested in joining him?"

"This isn't right," I heard Will mutter.

Finally, when we got to the top of the stairs, I heard a female security officer directing traffic.

"Ladies to the left, gentlemen to the right."

Veronica's hand slipped away from mine as we were separated by sheer force of the crowd. I was nearly pushed behind a black curtain where a male security guard was waiting.

"Lift your arms, please," he instructed. I tried to summon my inner Nameless strength and refuse, but he narrowed his eyes. "Are we going to have a problem here?"

I relented, not ready to deal with any kind of confrontation as the guy scanned me. "Are you Nameless?" he asked.

"No."

"Do you know who Nameless is?"

"No."

The officer then patted me down, and roughly. I was humiliated, overwhelmed, and my battery was completely drained. I hoped he didn't notice me panicking, because the last thing I needed was to be accused of lying. I mean, I was, but I probably couldn't stand up to more questioning.

"Next!" he yelled toward the front.

Speeding around to an empty corner, I collapsed against the wall, my breathing becoming more erratic. Crying, I hid my face in my knees. Was all of this my fault? Did I bring it on everyone? Did I cause Jesse to snap?

I turned my head to see Veronica, but she was whisked away in a human landslide. The masses were moving toward me, and I tried to collect myself and stand up.

Was this worth it? Was any of it worth it? What had I done?

MISS HUNTER

THE MANILA FOLDER SAT ON MY DESK. MY STUDENTS tapped their feet as everyone's discomfort reached a new level. Sitting at my desk, I couldn't help but feel the same way. Better now than never, I supposed.

"Before we begin class," I muttered regretfully, "I have been instructed by the police . . . and school security," I added with scorn, "to ask you this question: Does anyone in this classroom know who Nameless is?"

I beheld a sea of stoic faces. All except for one, but that was expected.

"I don't like that I have to ask you that," I continued. "I listen to the show too, and anyone who was outside the school before . . . the incident . . . knows that I had my disagreements with the methods of security enforcement, even before the stakes were raised."

One of my students shifted uncomfortably, but I noticed another staring directly at me with an accusatory flair.

"So why didn't you do something about it?" asked Mark, as if I had committed the act myself.

"I tried to," I said. "I was sent home for daring to suggest that a security officer should not be striking a student."

"This is like in the book," someone else mused. Will? Will read the book? Apparently everyone else was experiencing the same level of surprise I did, as they turned to hear him speak about this.

"I beg your pardon?" I asked.

"The part of the book where Charlie speaks the truth about how he feels about Mary Elizabeth," Will elaborated. "He loses everything for being honest."

"That's . . . very insightful, Will."

"And it's not until he stands up for his friends that people take notice of what's going on," Mark added. He got up, and walked straight over to Will and James. They both rose to greet him. Did they plan this?

"So what do we make of everything?" I said, shattering the moment to bring us back on topic.

"My dad says he'll suspend anyone who has any connection to Nameless," James groaned.

"So it's time we stand up for ourselves," Mark proclaimed. "Not just because of Nameless, but because it's like Nameless has been saying all along: There's something wrong here, and they're taking it out on us under the guise of our protection."

"But it only works if we let it happen," added Will.

"So what do we do?" asked Mark.

The three turned to me. I didn't know what to say. I was becoming a mere spectator at this point.

"We can't go and punch them in their faces," James admitted.

"But we can all stand up to this and let our voices be

heard," Will countered.

"They can't suspend the entire school," Mark agreed.

The entire class stood, as I almost expected to hear them say, "O Captain, my captain." I doubted any of them would get the reference.

Will stepped to the front of the class. "Are you with us?" he asked. The students roared in approval. He turned to . . . Mark, of all people. "Lead the way."

The throbbing mass of youthful energy coalesced as they left the classroom, leaving me alone. Well, me and one other student. The quiet, stoic one.

"You okay, Lucas?"

"Yeah, I guess," he responded, barely above a whisper.

"Are you worried?" I followed up, though I wasn't sure how anyone wouldn't be at this point.

He turned toward the door, and I acknowledged his gaze. The door. That door. The one where it happened. Where screams had rung out before, they echoed again, only this time, their purpose was unification. Resistance.

"I'm worried," he finally responded, "for them. I don't want things to get any worse."

"They have to," I said.

He turned to me, confused. Well, might as well teach one kid something. "They have to reach the breaking point before any change can occur. You should know that better than anyone."

Shit . . . I shouldn't have let that slip.

Lucas stiffened. "As big of a fan of *Hamlet* as you are," I added, hoping to ease the tension. "I would think you, of all people, would understand that."

"I guess we have to make sure that the sword isn't poisoned," he replied, going along with it—or just humoring me, perhaps. He finally headed out the door with the rest of his classmates.

Once he was out of reach, I added one more thing. The one I wished with all I had I could've said without terrifying the kid.

"Take back your own name."

JESSE

THE ROOM HAD BEEN DARK FOR 18 HOURS. I HADN'T been fed or spoken to a lawyer, nor was I expecting to. I fully believed that I would die here, a sacrifice to the cause. I didn't deserve to live, after all, as I might've taken a completely innocent life. What was there left to talk about?

Finally, the door creaked open, and a man in a suit and tie shuffled some papers and sat down across from me. The chair pulling out screeched like a banshee, and I covered my ears. He shot me an annoyed glance, as if that were unreasonable, and opened a manila folder. Staring for several seconds at the contents before he looked up at me again, he nodded while his glasses clung to the tip of his sweaty nose. How long had it been since this man had a blowjob?

"Jessica Parks?" he inquired.

"Jesse," I corrected.

"I'm only calling you what's on the file. Nicknames aren't necessary."

"It's not a nickname, it's my name," I insisted.

He slammed the folder down and put both his hands on the table, as if he was going to intimidate me. "I don't want to be here any more than you do," he snarled, "so the sooner you shut the fuck up, the sooner we can be done with this."

Shuffling through more papers, he waited to address me again. I gave him the silence he needed.

"Tell me what happened," he demanded quietly.

"I don't know," I honestly replied.

He scowled "Don't be a fucking idiot. Everyone saw what you did. I just want to know your side of the story so people don't think this is a witch hunt."

"What if it is?"

"Kid," he yelled, "you shot another student!"

"I know."

"Why did you do it?"

"I didn't mean to hit her!"

"Oh, that somehow makes it better?"

"Yes!"

"Why?"

My head hit the table before I could process what he was doing. I didn't have time for this shit, nor his overcompensation for the unease he felt at that moment. "I wanted Will."

"Will? The football kid?"

"Yes, the beloved, precious football player."

"Why? Everyone loves him."

"Not everyone."

"So because you didn't, you were going to shoot him?"

"No," I corrected. "I was going to shoot him for what he did to me."

"And what did he do to you that was worthy of death?"

"Actions beyond what I'm willing to tell you."

"Don't get smart with me, girl," he growled.

"I'm not a girl, sir," I insisted.

"Whatever. Rot in here for all I care. Point is, you shot a young girl, and you're going to jail either way. Only difference really will be if it's for murder or attempted murder." He stood up, slamming his chair into the table.

"She didn't deserve it," I replied, "but Will did."

"Why did you initially aim at James then?"

"He could've helped," I mused, "but didn't. Chose not to, despite what was going on. What had always been going on before, and happened again that day."

"Which was?"

"Fuck you, I'm not telling you anything," I snapped.

"I hope they throw away the key when they're done with you, girl," he threatened.

"Don't call me girl, sir!" I screamed.

"I'll call you whatever the fuck I want to call you. I don't take orders from scared little girls who shoot people!"

"I'm not scared, and I'm not a girl," I yelled back. "My name is Jesse. I'm a boy. I'm not scared, I'm regretful because I never meant to hurt her, but your prize boy down at the school who is being treated like a hero yet again? He deserves it . . . and so much worse. Now it'll never happen. Now you'll all treat him like some kind of legend. Just what he needed—more of an ego. Great. Just fucking great."

"Are ya done?" the officer snidely remarked.

"Yeah," I conceded. "Whatever."

The officer grabbed for the door, then turned back. "I'll send another officer in when she gets in," he explained. "She's generally better at dealing with these sort of feelings and womanly things."

"Thanks, Dick," I replied once he had shut the door.

Womanly things. What a charming, middle-aged man-child.

The clips on the television down the hall were still showing the school being evacuated, and then they focused on signs bearing the word "Nameless." The Voice? Is that what they were calling him now? The suits on the screen must've been talking about it. Were they gonna blame this on him too? Did I ruin everything for him?

I reclined on two legs of the chair, barely letting it not tip over. What difference would it make, anyway? Nobody was going to believe my story, regardless of what I told them, so why bother? Fuck it, fuck it all. But at least I could leave Nameless out of it.

VERONICA

LUCAS FOLLOWED THE SOURCE OF THE NOISE WITH SUCH a steely silence. For crying out loud, did this boy ever let himself feel good about something he accomplished? Or at least to which he contributed? Bringing him out of the weeds would be the death of me!

He opened the doors first, and instantly fell back as if pelted with snowballs upon arrival. I'd seen this behavior before, and I quickly rushed to catch him, wrapping my arms around the back of him and letting him know it was okay. Panic attacks, I guessed. The sounds were way too loud for him, so I steered him toward a quieter corner, but there was no escaping Dickhead Don and his trusty megaphone.

"Students, return to your classes immediately!" he commanded like someone who actually had a set. I was so sick of his jackass that I was ready to take that megaphone and . . .

"Isn't this great?" I quipped instead.

"Yeah, it's really, really great," he groaned, still partially covering his ears, and apparently completely oblivious to what was happening around him.

Police sirens started to whine in the distance, so I kept tugging him until we got to the football field, ironically the one quiet place on campus at this particular time. Remains of the chaos and riot from last night were still visible, including the speakers, ready for the Voice's next words to reach a student populace that had all had enough.

Lucas started freaking out, possibly due to the increased state of anxiety that normally comes with panic attacks, but I had to remain firm. "What's wrong?"

"This whole thing has gotten way out of control!" he cried, still in a state of fight-or-flight. I couldn't help but want to strangle him at the same time for not seeing the positives of what was transpiring.

"This doesn't have to end badly for anyone," Don's voice echoed even back here. "Just return to your classes peacefully!"

Great, he was already threatening us, and the leader of our resistance was too busy worrying about what was going to happen to see that we needed him now more than ever now.

Come on, Lucas! Be the Voice we know you can be!

"Of course it's out of control," I insisted. "Your words have finally been heard, and everyone is standing up. That's a good thing!"

Still pacing frantically, he ran his hand through his hair several times. "This is gonna get bad," he fretted. "I don't want to see anyone get hurt!"

"Come on, what's really wrong here?" He attempted to get away, but I remained in front of him. This needed to happen, and I wasn't going to let him run from it.

"This is what you wanted," I reminded him, "isn't it? That's why you've been doing the podcast all this time, right?"

"I didn't expect it to turn into a riot!" he exclaimed.

Pointing toward the crowd with a combination of pride and annoyance, my frustration had reached its limits. "Then what the fuck did you expect? Teatime and a peaceful negotiation? They're all standing up to a corrupt administration, one that has taken things to an extreme, and they're fighting back! This is what you encouraged them to do! They're listening to you, dammit! Listen!"

I continued pointing toward the crowd, though pointing to a sound was slightly awkward. But the unmistakable voices of unrest were not to be avoided, and he couldn't run from them forever. He'd started this, and now he needed to keep going. It was up to me to make sure Nameless didn't die. We had too many voices in our generation speak up until things got too difficult, and then conspicuously disappear.

Not this time, goddammit!

LIONEL

Our squad car pulled in, unmarked like the rest of them, and it seemed as if the entire student body was out front protesting. What had Don gotten himself into now?

"Sir!" one of the officers called to me, and I turned to give him assistance with coordination. We needed to make sure nothing got out of hand, lest it cause even more violence and bloodshed.

"Now," I heard Don command, "you can return to your classes, or the police can get involved, it's your decision."

He was threatening violence now, as if he commanded the entire police force. This was why power didn't need to be in the hands of someone like this, but right now, what choice did I have? Firing the security guard again would be a political nightmare, especially since so many people saw the connection between him being sent home and the kid bringing the gun to school.

Was Lucas involved in this? He was probably a

wreck from all the noise. I had to make sure he didn't get trampled, but looking through all the faces, I realized I didn't know a single one of his friends anymore.

Well shit, son, I hope you're okay. This is getting ugly.

LUCAS

THE COPS SURROUNDED THE KIDS. SOME OF THEM WERE even carrying riot shields. They weren't fucking around anymore, especially now that Dad was in charge. I didn't always like his approach, or his seemingly undying urge to compromise with corruption, but he was nothing if not effective. It was over. Nothing more could or would come from it.

"See," I said, pointing toward the organizing police force, "nothing's going to change. This has been pointless."

"It's not over, dammit!" Veronica shouted.

"It *is* over," I countered. "I can't go on again."

She looked at me incredulously. I couldn't tell if she was in love with me or plotting my death. "What the hell are you saying?"

"The show," I meekly responded. "It has to end before things get worse."

JAMES

I SUPPRESSED HEATHER'S CRIES IN THE DEPTHS OF MY mind. Now was not the time to be reminded of them. I had to be strong for her and strong against my father, whom until this moment, I had never defied. Would anyone ever forgive me?

"What the hell is going on here?" I heard a familiar voice demand.

I turned to see Principal Sawyer. Dad stood beside her after rushing to the first sign of intermediate authority, and I could tell I'd pissed him off. *Now or never, James. So many amends had to be made.*

"You think you can just walk out of school like that because you don't agree with something?" Principal Sawyer snarled at me.

Before I could answer, Mark and his new, shiny spine spoke up himself. "Pretty sure we have the right to do so, constitutionally and all."

"You're students!" Principal Sawyer unabashedly screamed. "You have the right to get back inside that school where you belong, or face the consequences!"

Will stepped up between both Mark and me. "We'd rather face the consequences of our actions than submit to having our rights taken away."

Will's presence loomed over everyone's, even Dad's, and it gave me a chance to quiet my guilt. Maybe all of this really was my fault. Would anyone ever talk to me again if they found out the truth?

DON

NAMELESS HAD CORRUPTED ALL THESE INNOCENT children and turned them into Satanic puppets. Even the quarterback was defying me now. This had to be stopped, even if force had to be used. I wasn't backing down.

"I expected better from a star quarterback," I chided.

"I expected better from all of you," he retorted.

That was it. Someone had to beat some sense into all of them. I grabbed him by the letter jacket and started trying to drag him toward the police commissioner. Surely he hadn't lost his mind in this nonsense yet.

"Commissioner," I called, barely able to move this kid but not showing weakness at the same time, "please help me remove these insubordinate students from campus."

"Are they connected to Nameless?" he inquired.

"They may as well be," I replied, annoyed that he even had to ask.

"I am Nameless!" someone else declared. Everyone else looked surprised at the source, and I turned to see, of all people, the little nerdy kid. Son of a bitch, it was you all along?

MARK

WHAT HAD I JUST SAID? COULD THIS BE USED AGAINST ME in a court of law? I knew my rights, but did I actually have to use them?

"*You're* Nameless?" the police chief asked me.

Nobody else was chanting yet, so I needed to be more obvious. Will and James continued staring at me incredulously, so it needed to have better rhythm to it. "I . . . am . . . Nameless!"

Chant it, goddammit! Chant it!

The police commissioner reached into his pocket, unhitching his handcuffs. *Shit, guys . . . say something. Say anything!*

"Well if that's the case . . ." the commissioner began.

"I am Nameless!" James announced.

JAMES

NOBODY WOULD EVER FORGIVE ME FOR WHAT I'D DONE once they found out, so I might as well help the best I could while I still had any credibility remaining.

"What did you say?" Dad growled.

"I am Nameless!" Will yelled.

DON

"I AM NAMELESS!"

All three of these thugs were chanting at me. Smacking the back of my son's head, which was less than he deserved, I turned to the authorities. "Get them out of here!"

"I am Nameless!" they continued to chant, foolishly believing that anyone else would risk their name and reputation to be associated with someone not even brave enough to reveal themselves.

"You were right, Don," Principal Sawyer conceded while watching with me. "I can't believe it's come to this."

A smile was creeping across my face, despite my best efforts to remain cool, but the victory over this arrogant bitch was so strong that I had to rub it in a little.

"I told you it would, Principal Sawyer," I gloated, perhaps a little too much.

"Yes, you did," she conceded. Victory! *Stupid bitch. Get back to the teaching position you were promoted from and let the men do the dirty work.* "Now find him and help me get things back to normal."

Woman thinks she can still boss me around? What does she think I am, anyway? Fuck her!

I slammed the front doors in her face, making sure she knew what I thought of her in the process, and the police commissioner came with me. Good, the men were handling shit now. Time to actually get some things done instead of worrying about all this political correctness and feelings and shit.

"Do I have your support, Commissioner?" I asked, knowing that my methods by now had to have proven themselves.

"You do, but I'll tell you one thing," he began, and he spun me around so that we were face-to-face. Fine. This was how men handled their business, instead of putting on a mask and hiding. I stood tall, even inching closer to his face, letting him know that he didn't scare me. This alpha wouldn't budge.

"What?" I whispered right in his face, daring him to disagree with me.

"Don't forget, I hired you," he whispered back, "and I can fire you just as easily as the principal did. Watch yourself."

"James deserved it for mimicking that stupid protest chant," I reminded him.

"Am I clear?"

Oh, he was gonna use the same tactic as the female principal now? Maybe he wasn't the man I thought he was. I was gonna have to handle this on my own, it seemed.

"Crystal clear," I replied with less respect than any

of these students had for me at the moment. That would change soon enough too.

VERONICA

I WASN'T LETTING HIM BACK OUT OF THIS. LUCAS reneging on everything I knew he believed could see us living under much worse circumstances than we already were. I couldn't let that happen.

"You can't just turn your back on everyone now!" I yelled again, trying to get through his thick fog of anxiety and fear. "People are counting on you!"

"This whole thing is insane," he repeated, as if my position on that were going to change. "I can't do this anymore!"

Goddammit, Lucas. You're really gonna make me do this, aren't you?

"You have to," I cried in his ear. "This is what you started!"

Taking several steps toward the school, I pointed one more time where he could see several students being dragged off by the cops. "Look what's happening! The students are rising up because they know as much as we do that this is all bullshit!"

I took a breath, hoping he'd relax a little bit and

look at things honestly and rationally instead of fearing what might happen to him. And me, possibly. I didn't know how he felt yet because he never spoke the fuck up about it!

"Yes, they went back inside when the cops arrived," I conceded, "but they'll be back. They'll be right here, waiting to hear from you tonight! You can't let them down, not after they've taken in all of your words and are now not only listening, but reacting!"

"They've shut down the Internet at school," he wearily reminded me. "How can I do this without being traced?"

Finally, an in! Even the cracks in your wall are sometimes visible, you goddamn lug!

I extended my hand toward him in my best "come with me if you want to live" manner.

"I have an idea . . ."

BRIAN

MARK, JAMES, AND WILL WERE ALL HERE, ALONG WITH Sean, Liz, and several others.

They'd kept their word: This was on.

LUCAS

WE DROVE WITH THE TOP OF VERONICA'S WHITE Pontiac down. The breeze blew through her hair, picking up the sunlight in her eyes, and I couldn't believe I'd never taken the time to look at her like this. She was so stunning. What on earth did she want with someone like me? How did I even still have a chance?

DON

MEETING, SOS. LIONEL HAD CALLED TOGETHER THE officers and security teams. Good, a plan to get this done with once and for all.

BRIAN

THE FOOTBALL TEAM REMOVED THE STAGE FROM THE football field, and Mark backed the truck up. They were all in. This was finally happening. Even when Nameless started speaking up, I couldn't believe we were all finally united instead of fighting over all the petty bullshit that goes on in high school. Whether or not I graduated at this point was superfluous—this was about our rights.

LUCAS

"NOBODY'S HOME," I WHISPERED, HOLDING THE DOOR open into the kitchen. "Go upstairs!"

NURSE

SIX P.M. CHECK, THE POOR GIRL WAS STILL UNCONSCIOUS. The flowers and cards would be so nice for her to wake up to, though. They took up almost the entire room at this point. Sweet kids.

MARK

THE BOYS WERE DOING ALL THE GRUNT WORK. I RAN checks on the equipment, and I wasn't seeing any resistance. That didn't mean anything right now, though. Once they figured out what was up, it would be the toughest cyber battle of my life. I had to be ready.

LIONEL

THE ENTIRE STREET—I COULDN'T BELIEVE IT. PLACARDS, bodies, messages everywhere. This was one of the finest demonstrations of the First Amendment I'd ever seen, and these were kids! So much of my generation lamented how they didn't care about anything anymore and were lazy, Internet-addicted punks. They should see this.

"I am Nameless!" was written on so many of them that I couldn't keep track.

These kids weren't idiots. None of their construction touched school property, but remained in public domain on the street, just outside the school zone.

My officers lined the back of the stage at a safe distance. I'd instructed them to be careful not to interfere with the students' First Amendment rights, as the last thing we needed was another scandal, and this one where we were the violators of constitutionality. Kids getting shot wasn't as big a deal as Columbine had made it a few years ago, so we didn't have that leg to stand on, either. This situation was delicate, and if I only had one nutcase to deal with in the school security guy, that was more than enough.

I watched him carefully, making sure he wasn't getting up to anything even worse. He had a goddamn nightstick in his hand. I couldn't wait to run background on this psycho, as I was sure he had an outstanding warrant somewhere, and I wasn't gonna let him get away with anything once I didn't need him anymore.

The news started setting up. That slick dude, Joe Manning, was out front, getting candids with the kids and everything. Some people sure knew how to take advantage of a fucking tragedy.

VERONICA

I HEARD THE VOICE. I HEARD *THE VOICE*. THERE, LIVE, right in front of me. Lucas changed from this scared little kid into the freedom fighter I knew he was. His eyes slid away from the screen and up to me, and every hair on my body stood on end. I wanted him more than I'd ever wanted another person in my life, and I had to make my move because I knew for sure he wouldn't.

Suddenly, his hands were on my chin, pulling me close. Once I stood, he wasn't much taller than me, but it was the perfect height for me to see something in him other than fear. Finally, deep within those crystal pools, I saw what I needed to—the spirit that had created this resistance movement lived inside those eyes.

Our lips touched . . . I'm not sure who initiated, but it didn't matter. We were drifting along space as time all at once stopped, and the microphone was left there to capture a voice no longer speaking.

His back hit the mattress first, and our lips stayed connected as we found each other in a new location. I didn't think he had any idea what he was doing, but for right now, it didn't matter. Nothing else mattered. I was in love with Lucas, despite myself, despite all the reservations I had about him standing up for himself. We were about to share each other before we showed the world that we weren't ready to back down.

Oh, my. This boy doesn't know what he's capable of, I thought, shivering as he ground against me. *Time to teach him a lesson of a different nature and change his entire world for the better.*

Our eyes connected once more, and nothing stood between us. His skin, though covered in goosebumps, was the smoothest I'd ever touched, and I felt safe in his grip. I normally wasn't the one seeking refuge in the arms of another, but I didn't know I'd ever wanted that until I felt it for the first time. Mom and Dad weren't what I would call affectionate, and Will was all about himself and getting it done as quickly as possible, both on the field and in the bedroom.

For the first time in my life, I truly felt passion and was able to share it with another person. This was beyond magical, and I needed time to freeze just a little bit longer so I didn't have to let it go.

MARTHA

IT DIDN'T SOUND LIKE ANYONE WAS HOME, BUT EVEN now, I didn't think Lucas could handle the sights and sounds of the protest. Lionel had told me nearly every registered student of Columbus Area High was in the streets, and I may not have known my boy as well as I used to, but big crowds and loud noises? No way. He was more likely reading *Hamlet* again rather than caught up in that melee.

Unless he was the Voice behind it all, but no . . . that couldn't be . . .

Could it?

I knocked after assuring myself that it couldn't be my sweet boy, even with all his troubles.

LUCAS

MOM! SHIT!

I stirred when I heard knocking on my bedroom door. Veronica was asleep under my right arm. Goddammit, goddammit, we were so screwed . . . only not in the fun way this time.

"Just a minute!" I helplessly yelled.

MARTHA

WHAT COULD HE POSSIBLY BE DOING IN THERE? IT WAS him, wasn't it? Wait until his father found out. But could I tell on my baby like that? Did I have to? Would I be arrested if I didn't?

"Let me in right now!" I demanded in my best Mom voice. He'd know if he was in any trouble that this was the time to stop it and come out. He might not talk anymore, but he still respected me.

"Mom, this isn't a good time," I heard from the other side of the door.

Like hell it isn't.

"Open this door right away!"

Dammit, Lucas, this was the last thing this family needed. Everything was going so well. Even with your resistance to therapy and everything, you stayed out of trouble.

"I can't, not right now!" he cried back.

Busted, so hard he was busted, and I was going to wring his neck and drag him to the fields myself so his father could see the boy he was looking for.

216

I banged on the door again. "I knew it was you!" I informed him so he wouldn't even have the chance to lie. "Stop hiding and open up this instant! Now I've got . . ."

But then the door opened.

LUCAS

GLANCING BACK HELPLESSLY AT VERONICA, I UNLOCKED the door. She had just come to, but was safely under the comforter.

"Now I've got . . ." I heard my mom as I opened the door, but then she stopped. As I lifted my eyes to meet hers, she turned every shade of red there was.

"Oh," she sputtered. "You weren't broadcasting . . . Nameless . . ."

I tried to correct her, but I was probably as embarrassed as she was. I'd been caught with my pants down, literally.

"Hi, I'm Veronica," I heard from the other side of the room. Seriously? She was gonna do this now?

"Hi . . . Veronica . . ." Mom stammered to the best of her ability. "What were you . . . ?"

Veronica didn't miss a beat. "I was taking a nap," she lied. "The crazy protests at school had me worn out."

Oh, you beautiful girl who has chosen me for some reason, how often have you gotten out of sticky situations like this? Wait, bad choice of words . . .

"So you weren't . . . ?" Mom started to reply.

"We didn't have anything to do with them," she cut her off with the answer. "Don't worry."

If I believed in a heaven, I'd have sworn I had an angel sent to me for this very moment. Thank heavenly fuck . . .

Dammit Lucas, you have to work on these word choices in awkward situations!

MARTHA

I BREATHED A HUGE SIGH OF RELIEF. *NOT MY SON,* I thought happily. *Not my son.*

"Well, you have no idea how happy I am to hear that, and to meet you," I added, making sure Lucas knew I was happy to see he was socializing, even if this wasn't appropriate for someone his age.

Better this than the alternative . . . I think.

"I was afraid my son was that Nameless guy," I added, making sure they didn't think my intrusion was about . . . that.

"No worries at all," the sweet girl responded. "We've been here the whole time."

Be still, my heart. My son had a good girl! Thank God!

"I'm so relieved to hear that!" I proclaimed.

Walking back into the hallway, breathing easier and more embarrassed than anything that I'd suspected my son of such deeds, I tried to offer another olive branch while I had him in my sight and he wasn't arguing.

"If you two get hungry," I said, "there's leftovers in

the fridge."

The door closed behind me. Those cute kids, they weren't anything to worry about. Finally, I could be a happy mom again.

VERONICA

"TALK MUCH?" I ASKED WITH A GIGGLE.

Lucas shook his head vigorously, still redder than the deepest sunburn I'd ever seen. "I'm not exactly the best conversationalist under pressure."

I grinned. "What would you do without me?"

JOE MANNING

HELLO, COLUMBUS. IT'S TIME FOR THE BEST-LOOKING man in show business to give you the tragedy porn you all want. Anchor desk, here I come!

"This is Joe Manning, Columbus Evening News," I began with my trademark toothy smile, "here at Columbus Area High School."

These fucking idiots were helping my prospects without even knowing it. What a bunch of special snowflakes.

"As you can no doubt see," I opined, "literally hundreds of students . . ." *Or rather, children throwing a tantrum.* ". . . have lined the street in front of the campus, not only protesting the new security measures implemented in the wake of the recent shooting, but to show solidary with the anonymous podcaster ironically only known as Nameless."

That's right kids, you keep being anonymous. I'll take all the credit. Idiots.

I watched the head of security raise himself in a scissor jack with his megaphone like he was directing riot practice, or something. I needed to get out of these damn small towns and start covering something relevant already.

"Both the students and the administration are holding fast in their positions. The students have gathered here to exercise their First Amendment rights, but should anything get out of control . . ." *And it would.* ". . . the police are standing by."

Thank god.

"The one known as Nameless continued to broadcast last night, despite demands that he discontinue his show and turn himself in for questioning for his role . . ." *You know, causing the whole thing.* ". . . in the incident earlier this week. It was discovered he had been using the school's Internet services . . ." *Fucking freeloader.* ". . . to circumvent the tracing process, but with the entire system shut down at the behest of Principal Sawyer, his protection is no longer."

Time to take it home. It's Joe Manning Day, bitches!

"Now, the only question on everyone's mind: Will Nameless broadcast tonight, knowing that his location will be traced?"

Joe Manning, you slick son of a bitch, this has broadcast TV written all over it!

DON

ANIMALS. ALL OF 'EM. FUCKING ANIMALS.

I raised the megaphone from my position of safety. "Students, this has gone on long enough! If Nameless comes on tonight, he will be discovered. Law enforcement is now treating this as a hostile situation, so I would not advise anyone be seen aiding him in any way."

Or you'll go to jail with the rest of the criminals.

"Now . . ." I began again, but then the megaphone stopped working.

What the hell? Cheap Chinese-manufactured piece of shit . . .

"Hi Don," that voice came from over the speakers. "I heard you've been looking for me."

Joke's on you, kid. We'll find you before you finish gloating!

JAMES

A PART OF ME FELT BAD FOR LAUGHING AT DAD'S misfortune, but he'd gone totally off the deep end with this one. His face glowed red like it'd been left in the sun for too long, and he smacked the megaphone against the steel railing. Yeah, like that'd help.

The cheers surrounding us should've indicated where both voices stood, respectively. I doubted Dad would see it that way.

"They want me to come forward for my role in supposedly encouraging Jesse to go off the deep end and shoot an innocent girl," Nameless proclaimed, "or as if anything I could've said would've provoked him into doing something he wouldn't have done anyway. Why don't we ask Don what this is really about?"

Oh, shit, Nameless was throwing down tonight. Dad was going to have a fucking meltdown!

"They want me to reveal my identity and rob you of yours," Nameless said. "They've brought security to levels that would make the TSA blush! They're patting everyone down, treating us all like we're in Columbus

Area Maximum Security Prison, but they act like *I'm*
the one who's causing all the trouble. They want me to
reveal my name? Well, they know my name. You know
my name . . ."

"I am Nameless!" I shouted with the rest of the
students.

LIONEL

I HAD TO GIVE THIS KID CREDIT—HE CERTAINLY DIDN'T lack courage.

"Start the trace," Don commanded as if he had the power to authorize such things. "I hope they lock this kid up."

"And who is in charge of all this?" Nameless inquired. Curious to see what he thought of all this before we found him, I listened. He had a way of speaking that captured even those who were against him. Perhaps he had a future in broadcast journalism, if he didn't manage to get himself slapped with felony charges first.

"A power-hungry security officer who didn't have what it took to become a real cop," answered Nameless. I couldn't help but snicker a bit. "He takes it out on every single one of you. This is probably the guy who gave the A/V kids wedgies and swirlies when he was in high school, and now he can't understand why every chick at the local bar isn't throwing their panties at him."

I was chuckling aloud by this point. This kid was hilarious!

A loud crash interrupted my enjoyment as Don's megaphone shattered on impact from the scissor jack above. *Way to show that tempered anger, Don. Keep it up.* Even his own kid was smiling now.

"We're running it now," one of my officers informed me. Shame, but I still had to do my job.

"They can't stop all of you," Nameless informed the mob. "They can't suspend all of you. You know why?"

Do tell, kid.

"If they did, they'd have no one left to bully," he finished.

Snap, you brave soul! Fucking snap!

"They can expel a student," he continued. "They can expel five. Hell, they can expel every student that Don has put on his list of Undesirables!"

I figured I'd better get rolling on this before Don started thinking he had the privilege of shooting to kill.

BRIAN

THE CLAWS WERE OUT TONIGHT! I KNEW HE WOULDN'T
let me down!

Don was lowering in his stupid fucking scissor jack,
and I was there to smile and wave at him. He couldn't
touch me now—not on public property. The more
everyone laughed, the more it made him self-destruct.
Might as well keep it up!

Finally, someone in this fucking world was
standing up for us. Beside me stood Will and James.
Who'da thought we'd ever see the day where the jocks
stood by the Undesirables like us?

"It's their cherry-picking of which students deserve
to be saved that led to this powder keg exploding,"
Nameless declared, "though they'll likely misinterpret
that as a bomb threat."

*No shit, man. They'll do anything to get rid of the
ones they don't want. Maybe next they can expel
students for their income levels or bad looks.*

"Zero-tolerance, go fuck yourself!" Nameless said,
and the crowd went apeshit. I nearly broke into tears

myself. This was so surreal. The world that hated me a week ago now stood with me. I couldn't help but reflect on the time where I listened to the show alone, and now, here stood the entire school.

That shady news douchebag plugged his ears from all the cheering. *Poor guy, I hope he makes it home okay! Wouldn't want to lose any of the pomade he slathered his hair with!*

Don now jumped in front of me like a ninja on some sort of secret mission. "Get your criminal ass out of my way!" he screamed in my face. I smiled right back in his, waiting for his head to explode like Nameless' powder keg.

"We're not on school property," I reminded his impotent ass. "You have no power here!"

The police sirens screeched and two cars took off, momentarily distracting me from gloating in the discount rent-a-cop's face.

"They've found him now," Don said with a smirk. "Whoever he is, this is his last show."

He reached to his side pocket and pulled out a nightstick like some goddamned lunatic. "And as for you . . ." he began, "I've got my own bone to pick with you. I'm not a rent-a-cop!"

He started to raise it, but of all people, James stood in front of me. "I'm not gonna let you hurt anyone else!"

This was *Twilight Zone* shit! The others in our group embraced arms and stood between me and Don, linking a protective chain around me. Finally, they'd noticed. Finally, I was no longer an invisible blip on the school's radar.

Goddammit, Nameless, I'm not supposed to cry in

public! I have an image to uphold!

"This . . . this . . ." Don stammered, obviously as amazed as I was. "We'll see about this!"

LIONEL

WINDOWS SHATTERING DISTURBED MY ENJOYMENT OF Nameless' rhetoric. Things were getting out of control. I turned toward the school. Someone had spray-painted "I am Nameless!" on a brick and hurled it through.

What sounded like a battering ram turned out to be my unmarked car in the crowd getting rocked, and a few kids pushed it completely over like a tipped cow in the field. The car alarm turned some cheers into screams. Noise triggers. This shit was getting too real.

My fellow officers watched on, not sure what they were supposed to or allowed to do. I was right there with them. I needed a plan.

"They're not going to listen unless you take back the control," Nameless said, provoking the already-turbulent crowd. "Do what you want, make them feel uncomfortable for a change, don't let them subdue you!"

Will—perfect! Surely he could be rational about this. I grabbed his jacket and he turned around, ready to fight.

"Get off me," he growled.

"Will," I said, hoping to make peace, "you need to look around. You need to think about what could happen to these students. The officers with riot gear are on their way, and this crowd is getting out of hand."

"And this is my problem how?" he snapped back.

"Think about what will happen to all of these students if the officers start setting off tear gas or mace," I warned him.

That seemed to get his attention, but was it too late to do anything about it?

VERONICA

THE OFFICERS ARRIVED JUST IN TIME WITH THE CUE. I quickly uploaded it on my laptop and closed the site.

One of them opened the door. "Nameless, you're under arrest!" Ah, the hero was here to save the day!

Everyone looked around, confused, just as they ought to. This guy thought Nameless would be in here with a goddamn nametag or something.

"There, that's a Columbus student." One of the officers pointed at me. All right, time for a little click!

"Did I forget to mention this episode was pre-recorded?" Nameless' voice would ask at that very moment.

Podcast submitted, read the screen. I clicked out of it before the officer reached me. "Is there a problem, Officer?" I asked, feigning innocence and surprise.

"Have you seen Nameless around here?"

"What?" I responded, aghast. "I'm not sure what you're talking about."

"The podcast guy," he insisted. "Everybody knows! We traced the signal from his podcast to this building!"

"Sorry, Don," Nameless said over the walkie-talkie. "You'll have to get your rocks off by beating something else this evening."

"I don't know anything about a podcast," I added in my daintiest little voice.

"Apprehension negative," the officer stated in his walkie-talkie. "He must've used the free Wi-Fi in the restaurant and left."

"They can't stop all of you," Nameless reminded everyone. "Go fucking nuts. There's more of you than there are of them!"

I smiled, shut my laptop, and left the restaurant on the other side. Mission: accomplished.

JAMES

I HATED HEIGHTS, BUT THERE I WAS UP IN THE SCISSOR jack with Will. Even now, I couldn't stop thinking about what had happened to lead us to all of this, and I didn't mean Nameless.

Another window crashed and I began to panic. What if we were next? Will was trying to calm people down, but these kids were going insane!

Someone set a couch on fire in the yard, one from the faculty lounge, I guessed. The riot cops arrived in their black van, but a bonfire in the street was blocking their way. This was some new world order shit, and I, for one, was terrified.

The cheers rose up as the resistance refused to make way. They were so loud that I couldn't even hear myself think. That was probably a good thing, given what was happening in my head.

LUCAS

THE GLOW FROM WHAT I COULD ONLY IMAGINE WAS A bonfire on the street made my face visible in the mirror.

"Burn it all," I whispered in my best Heath Ledger voice. "Burn it to the ground."

Sometimes, the only way to cure something was to destroy it completely.

LIONEL

"LOOKS LIKE WE'LL HAVE TO CALL IN THE EXPERTS," I mused aloud. No one could've heard me over the riot, anyway.

JAMES

I STOOD OUTSIDE THE GLASS BOOTH. I WASN'T SURE WHY I was there, or what I hoped to accomplish, but something told me I needed to be there—for Heather, for Nameless, and for anyone else who had been swept up in this chaos.

The beep sounded, and he walked through the door. He sat down on the other side of me with a stone-cold gaze, not even giving me a second's worth of surprise or regard.

"Hi, Jesse," I meekly greeted him.

"What the fuck do you want?" he sneered. I couldn't blame him. Was I there for him, or the guilt that wouldn't go away? Could I even tell the difference between the two anymore? Probably not.

"I came to see how you were doing," I lied. "I don't imagine you get many visitors here." I tried to smile, but it was forced, and even he could see that.

"Cut the shit, James. Why are you here?"

"Well . . ." I stammered, looking for the right words. Were there any right words? I deserved to be in that hospital bed, not Heather. And yet here I was, with the person who put her there, trying to claim some of the responsibility, perhaps?

"I didn't know if you'd been following what was going on . . ."

"You mean how I ruined the school?" he sarcastically remarked. "You mean how all of you *finally* noticed something was wrong once someone got shot?"

"Not just that," I replied, "but that maybe there were other things that led to it. But Nameless is taking the fall, the blame."

"No, I am," he corrected. "Nameless is the token figure they can blame so that they don't have to look for the real problem."

"I know."

Jesse snorted. "How the hell would you know? What the hell do you know about anything?"

"You're right," I sputtered, realizing this wasn't going the way I hoped it would. Or maybe it was and I wasn't willing to acknowledge it. Either way, it was awkward.

"Finally, things got pushed to a head that forced the rest of you to take time out from making some of us miserable. What a shock that they aren't looking into what may have caused it other than an anonymous voice daring to speak up. I suppose it's easier than the truth."

"Which truth?" I asked, immediately regretting that. I knew from his tone he was alluding to the same thing I was trying to avoid.

"What, did you come here to pretend that what

happened didn't?" he demanded. "Did you really think that maybe if you made nice to me, I'd forget that you're part of why I'm here? Just because you and Will got your heads out of your asses for two seconds doesn't change what happened."

"No, it doesn't," I helplessly agreed.

"Then why . . . are you . . . here?"

"Two minutes," the guard warned.

Standing up, I started to head toward the exit, knowing that continuing this conversation would only make it worse.

"Do you remember that night, James?" he called out.

"What night?" I lied again.

"What night," he repeated with disgust. "Are you really that fucking stupid?"

"No."

"Of course you're not. You're smart enough to remember what it was like to pin my wrists down. You're smart enough to remember what it was like hearing me scream 'no!' despite what Will was doing to me. You're smart enough to remember that you may not have committed the act, but you're just as responsible."

"I'm sorry," I said.

He exploded "Sorry?! For what? That you two took what I can never get back? Or . . ." He smirked a little bit, which terrified me. ". . . were you hoping that the androgynous kid who looked familiar wasn't actually me? Were you hoping your ghosts from the guilty conscience you try to disregard would go away if it wasn't me?"

"No."

"Of course not," he continued, "you're not that dumb. You wish you were, though. Is that why you're here?"

"I just want to make things right," I pleaded.

"For you, or for everyone?" he asked as the guard pointed to his watch.

"Both!"

The guard started pulling Jesse away by the arm. "Put yourself on the line for them! It's too late for me."

"It *is* too late," the guard agreed. "Time's up."

"Jesse!" I screamed.

"My name was never Jessica!" he bellowed as he disappeared behind the beeping security door.

"I know," I responded, despite the fact that he was gone. "I'm sorry."

LIZ

DESPITE THE CHAOS, I FOUND SOME SMALL SENSE OF peace within myself by being who I was, who I'd hidden this whole time. Sean walked beside me as an ally, not as someone desperately trying to get back what he never had. That was admirable, especially given the circumstances, but he never once criticized it. What was there to criticize? I was gay. That wasn't in regard to him. It had nothing to do with him.

A hand suddenly grabbed me by the back of the shirt. "What the fuck?" Sean said.

"Sean!" I screamed.

"Shut up," an unfamiliar voice commanded.

We were dragged around the corner and brought to kneel before Zod, otherwise known as Deputy Don. I was sure they threw us down just so he would know what it was like to have a woman on his knees in front of him.

"Here are two more of your Nameless kids," the security officer guffawed.

"Indeed," Don agreed, not taking his eyes off us.

Don hooked an arm around each of us and led us to the front of the school.

"What the hell is this?" I demanded.

"You messed with the bull," he responded. "You got the horns."

Who the hell was he, Richard Vernon? "We didn't do anything," Sean pleaded.

"You were seen there last night," Don retorted. "We know you have connections to Nameless. You can get out with the others."

"Who? The whole school?" Sean replied.

We reached the front stairway and Sean slipped on the first step, nearly pulling us all down, but Deputy Don was even stronger than he looked.

"Why don't you two go find your criminal gang," he instructed with snark that even I could detect, "and maybe you can have a poetry reading with your favorite Nameless limericks?"

"Why don't you go fuck yourself?" Sean suggested. Damn, when did he get a spine like that? If I wasn't gay, I might've been attracted to him again.

Crack! Don's fist landed right on Sean's jaw, and a group of uniformed guards surrounded us both. One of them took him away and I tried to help Sean up.

Goddammit, this was going too far! I started thrashing after Don the best I could, but I wasn't getting anywhere. They weren't letting me through.

Fuck you, Don!

VERONICA

I RACED OUT THE DOOR WHEN I HEARD THE COMMOTION. Lucas stood there, observing.

"What's going on?" I asked him, hoping it wasn't as bad as I thought it would be.

"Don hit another student," he informed me, "and it looks like things just got serious." He paused. "Well, more serious."

What had to be an agent, as he had his hair slicked back and wore a suit, brushed past us and disappeared into the crowd, clearly on a mission. "Shit," I whispered.

"What are we gonna do now?"

MISS HUNTER

A GLASS OF MERLOT WOULD'VE BEEN GREAT RIGHT about then.

Only about ten students remained in my class. This was the new school. The secure school. The one with the undesirables removed. At least the ones they'd caught.

"If security keeps throwing kids out of school, I'm not gonna have a class left," I observed out loud.

Lucas wasn't staring back at me, but at the flowers on Heather's desk. I couldn't bring myself to look at them, even now. The specter of that crime hung over all of us, and it was getting worse by the second.

"I don't know what they expect is going to happen," I continued. "I'd say what's on my mind, but that's probably a suspense-worthy offense by now. Punishable by imprisonment, if certain people got their way."

Stepping away from the desk, I paced. What did it matter now? What did any of it matter if they were going to take every last one of us away until they got

247

what they wanted?

"We've been reading a book about a kid who writes anonymous letters," I desperately tried to connect what was going on to the assignment at hand, as if anyone was actually listening at this point. "He changes his name, and finds that writing to someone who doesn't know who he is becomes more therapeutic than a journal could ever be. He bonds with others, falls in love, goes through some of the worst times of his life, but always has that place to vent . . . to be honest . . . to let things out . . . To be, dare I say . . . Nameless." I dropped the word, knowing full well that could get me fired through association.

I looked toward the door, half-expecting Don to burst through with a gun to protect the sanctity of the school by killing those he didn't like. Nothing surprised me anymore.

"You take from that what you will," I continued. "Hell, maybe the real Nameless is sitting in here right now . . ."

But I did know. Did he know that I knew? Did it matter? I had his eyes on me, but I didn't want to blow his cover.

"And if he is," I said, "I'd tell him to never stop. No change has ever come from compliance with oppressors. Someone has to stand up for those who can't do it for themselves, and the fear it's bringing out speaks volumes about what they've been trying to do around here."

The bell clanged. Shit, it was probably relief at this point. What else could the marking of the end of the countdown be? I glanced toward the class, expecting them to scurry away like they always did, but they remained sitting for some reason. None of them moved.

"It's okay, you can go now," I said, releasing them from their term in this class, possibly for the last time.

"Please," Lucas replied, "finish."

Several more students backed him up. This was not expected, and I felt like I was on the spot. "I don't know what I've got left to say," I admitted. "Who knows how many of us will even be here after this weekend? It's Friday, go home."

Nobody moved. This was probably going to get me fired too. I was fired eight different ways from Sunday, surely.

"Kids, I don't want this to get any worse for you," I sighed. "It probably can, but I don't want to find out. If you want to, write me a letter just like Charlie did. That's probably the only way we can get out what we truly need to say."

"When's it due?" a student inquired, because of course they did.

"Just get it to me whenever," I answered. "Or not. This has gone beyond what school should ever expect any of you. Enjoy your weekend. I hope all, or any, of us are back on Monday."

PRINCIPAL SAWYER

"Got rid of two more of those . . ." Don said as he entered my office, but his steps stopped along with whatever else he was going to say. I knew what that was.

"Aw, shit," he muttered instead.

Lionel stood behind me. I couldn't see through the hands covering my aching head, but it didn't matter. I heard the handcuffs being removed from his pocket, and I didn't want anything to do with the moment. Things were more deeply screwed up than I ever thought they could be, and I wanted it to end more than anything.

"What are you doing?" Don asked.

"I warned you, Don," Lionel said. He shoved Don up against the door he came in through, nearly knocking it off its hinges with the force.

"You struck a student, Don," I reminded him. "You had my support on this one, and you blew it."

"Extreme measures call for extreme reactions!" he cried.

Lionel struggled with him. Even a man of his size could've been overpowered by the brick shit house Don was. "Your job was to find Nameless, not to start throwing kids out of school, and certainly not to punch them. You're under arrest for assault, and we're going to look into your activities as far back as grad school."

Just end it already, I silently pleaded, but Don getting crazy strength woke me out of my stupor. He leaned Lionel back against the wall, causing him to break the hold before the handcuffs were closed.

"Hell with this! Hell with you both!" he screamed. "I'll take care of this myself!"

Before Lionel could recover, Don burst through the office door and ran down the hallway. Lionel tried to follow, but he was already gone. He moved fast for someone his age, even in that kind of shape. Lionel pulled out his hand radio.

"This is the commissioner," he said to the officers on the other end of the line. "If you see the Columbus security guard, Mr. Donald Kasich, you are to arrest him on sight. Repeat, you are to arrest him on sight!"

Lionel sighed and then looked back at me, as if I had anything left to contribute. "I'm sorry," I said. "I should've never let him back in here."

"You didn't," Lionel corrected me. "I did." He straightened his jacket and strode toward the door.

"Mr. Commissioner," I called after him.

"Yes?" he answered, turning back to me over his shoulder.

"I'd feel better if you stuck around," I admitted. "Between Nameless still being at large and now Don doing God knows what, some order around here would be welcomed."

"Not to worry," Lionel said.

Four agents, all in pressed suits with shiny hair, surrounded him as if he'd lit up the FBI's version of the Bat Signal.

"I see you called in backup."

"If Nameless goes on the air again, we'll have him in no time flat," Lionel explained. "At this juncture, we now have to hope we'll find him before Don does."

"You don't think he'd . . ." I started.

"The man is a loose cannon," the head agent said. "He's capable of anything."

The four moved out with Lionel leading the way. This had gotten way more out of control than I could've ever imagined. It seemed like only weeks ago that my school was content and invisible. How I wished for those days again when the worst problem I had was the coffee machine not working properly.

VERONICA

HE WAS LOST IN HIS OWN HEAD AGAIN. I KNEW WHAT HE was thinking, but I needed to get it out of him anyway.

"So are you going to go on tonight?" I inquired.

His face was aghast, as if I'd suggested a murder-suicide pact. "Are you nuts? Did you see those guys my dad brought in?"

"Did you see what happen to Sean?" I replied. The words seemed to slip from me of their own accord.

"How am I supposed to go on?" he cried. "They'll find me before I can finish the intro!"

"It doesn't matter if they find you!" I tried to shout sense into him. "Don't you understand?"

"No, I don't!"

"Of course you don't!" My righteous brain took over. "All this time, you've been encouraging everyone to rise up and take back their name, but you can't even do that yourself, can you?" Fuck, I was ruining any chance I'd ever had with him, wasn't I?

"This is on a federal level now," he reminded me. "Who knows what'll happen if they find out who I am?

They could lock me away with Jesse!"

"And if you don't," I began, "fuck it, right? All those people who are listening, those for whom you've become the Voice—fuck them, right? They'll be down there waiting for you, and you won't do anything about it, will you?"

I caught my breath, then out of pure instinct, hugged him to stop him from withdrawing further into himself. I think that surprised him more than anything.

"What was that for?" he asked.

Sighing, I realized I might never get through to this thick-headed goddamned prodigy. "You are so oblivious sometimes," I said, starting to storm away.

I didn't expect him to follow. I thought he'd watch me leave, like every other time we'd gotten in this position, but he chased me down.

"So what do we do?" he asked.

"You figure it out," I snapped. "If you want to blow everyone else off tonight, you go right ahead." I sped up, leaving him in the dust.

"Where are you going?" he called after me.

"To be let down with the rest of them," I sneered in an effort to strike a chord. His footsteps got close to me for a second, but then I saw him grab both of his temples. Another panic attack, but I couldn't help him. Not this time. He needed to rise up all on his own.

Then, as if a lightbulb went off in his beautiful goddamn brain, he stopped on a dime and sped off in another direction. Wanting to chase after him desperately, I instead let him go. *Let's see what he can do without me pushing him to be brave.*

But the question was, for me at least, could I still be?

PRINCIPAL SAWYER

THEY WERE PUTTING UP A STAGE NEAR CITY HALL. Barricades were set up like it was the scene of an oncoming riot. I was at protests in the 80s that weren't this well coordinated. Dozens of them were already waiting. All of this . . . for an anonymous kid talking? Maybe I'd never get it.

The agents followed Lionel and me into the building. It was probably the closest I'd ever get to feeling like the Secret Service was tailing us.

"We've got to get the mayor in on what's happening," Lionel said.

"Before this all goes wrong," I added.

We turned a corner, and I heard a voice coming out of a partially-opened door. It sounded like . . . but no, it couldn't have been . . .

MISS HUNTER

I'D NEVER THOUGHT I'D SEE THE DAY WHERE THE KIDS wanted to come to school on a Friday night, but here we were; all of us, learning together, before we'd find out if Nameless would go on the air.

My collection of students who had been tossed— Brian, James, Will, Mark, Liz, Sean, and many others who had been thrown away by Don—sat in a circle with their desks facing me. Someone had to educate these kids, and the school was certainly no longer interested in doing so.

Predictably, the door slammed open, revealing Principal Sawyer and the police commissioner. I knew they'd get here sooner or later, so I turned to them with my best teacher voice. "Can I help you, Joyce?"

"That's Principal Sawyer to you now," she growled. I got a giggle out of how much her words came back to bite her this time around. She had the chance to stop everything, but instead gave the keys to a madman. No forgiveness. "What in God's name are you doing here, Miss Hunter?"

"I'm giving these kids an education, since your security deemed them unworthy of it." I threw some shade at her tightly bound lips. "Do you mind?"

"I absolutely do mind! Don might've been out of line in his methods, but these kids are all involved with Nameless."

"They're just kids, Joyce," countered the commissioner.

"You stay out of this," she barked at him. That wouldn't end well. He was still the police commissioner. She wasn't on school grounds anymore.

Brian stood up and interrupted their little tiff. "You didn't do anything when Don ran us out of school."

James joined him. "You let him back in after everything he did," he added. "After everything you saw him do."

"After he threw us out for standing up for ourselves," Will proudly added.

"So we found a way to continue our education," Mark continued.

"And we're going to be listening to the show tonight," snickered Liz.

"Because the school let us down," said Sean. "The police let us down, but Nameless never will."

"If Nameless goes on the air tonight," Lionel indignantly replied, "we will find him."

Principal Sawyer stepped closer to me, as if she had anything left with which to intimidate me. "End this," she snarled, "or your time with Columbus is over."

"You can't fire me for working with local kids on public property," I reminded her. "What are you gonna fire me for, doing my job?"

Every vein in her forehead was about to burst. I no longer cared what she thought or what she'd do. "Your job is to each the students who are responsible enough to not be thrown out of school," she hissed.

How clueless was this woman? Before everything happened, she at least seemed to be a rational counter to Don's insanity. Now, I didn't know who was who anymore, but I did know none of these kids deserved to be kicked out of school, and that was enough for me.

Fuck her. She had no power over me anymore.

"And your job is to not let a crazed psycho take over your school and tell you who has the right to a goddamned education." I hoped that made her snap. Just give her a reason to do what I knew she would. She no longer had the fortitude to do what was right, so I didn't need her or anyone else who was falling for this bullshit.

"I'll send you your things in the mail," she snipped.

"Get the hell out of my classroom," I demanded to her face. "I have a lesson to finish.

Her face shifted several different shades of red. Then she finally left, Lionel following her and trying to keep her from returning.

PRINCIPAL SAWYER

I'D ALWAYS ENVISIONED MYSELF BECOMING THE principal in *Lean on Me*, but it seemed more like I was the mayor now. I stood with the megaphone, but rather than shouting for my rights against the popular demand, they wanted my head on a stake.

The news cameras were everywhere. Kids filled the area with their signs, and they had speakers set up for several blocks. I stood, the police and agents backing me up, and tried to walk out on stage to address them. Their boos made it very clear where they stood. I didn't have an ally left.

"Students," I began, "we have federal agents involved with this. If Nameless goes on with a podcast for you, he will be apprehended and shamed for all of you to see. I suggest you go home, and end your association with this cowardly, anonymous instigator immediately!"

Something had caught their attention, because I was no longer hearing the verbal threats and comments hurled in my direction. The crowd began parting, and they fell silent as someone walked toward the stage.

"Who is that?" I asked, as surprised as anyone. "Is that Nameless?"

LIONEL

"No," I REPLIED, AS STUNNED AS SHE WAS. "No, IT ISN'T."

The figure reached the stage, stepping up to Principal Sawyer and away from the crowd. I sure wasn't going to interfere with this. I was as curious as ever what they had to say.

They turned to the crowd, and a huge ovation erupted from all of them. How could they not? Heather was alive and standing here in front of us.

"You'll have to forgive me for interrupting you," she began, "but I have something to say."

She snatched the megaphone from Principal Sawyer's hands like Joyce herself probably had grabbed many a cellphone in her day. Joyce started to resist, but I pulled her back. If anyone deserved to have their opinion heard, it was Heather.

"I've been hearing endless words about whose fault it is about what happened to me, about how I should be feeling, and about what I should be doing," she began.

"Put down the megaphone," Principal Sawyer urged. I tried elbowing her to get her to stop. She'd lost all touch with reality if she wasn't going to let this girl speak.

"I've been hearing that it's Nameless' fault that Jesse shot me," Heather continued. "But the last time I checked, Jesse was detained, and yet Nameless has still been going on the air."

Joyce reached for Heather one more time, and I had one of the agents grab her behind the arms. "I want to hear what she has to say," I admitted to her.

"But she . . ."

Finally, I verbally smacked her the way I should have done days ago. "Shut up."

"Jesse is the one who shot me, not Nameless," Heather said. "Nameless is the one who has been the Voice. The Voice for all of us, to all those like this principal would rather have us be subjected to and humiliated in front of, just so that something like this doesn't happen again. Don't you see that? Those of you trying to hunt him down, don't you understand that he's trying to show you there's something wrong here?"

She had the crowd in the palm of her hand like no one I'd ever seen. This girl was going to be a star one day, and she'd point to this moment as the impetus, I had no doubt. What a story she had to tell!

VERONICA

THE SUSPENDED SIX STOOD WITH ME, BUT I COULDN'T hold back anymore. We jumped on stage, the rest of them following me, and I embraced Heather, trying not to hold too tight. She'd been shot recently, after all.

"I can't believe you're here!" I said.

"I *am* here," she replied. "And I'm still alive. Don't act like I'm already dead to further your own agenda. I'm here because Will and Lucas acted quickly, not because Nameless inspired anyone to hurt me. Though Will, I suppose it's only fair that you take responsibility for your role in that incident, don't you think?"

Will nodded shamefully. What role? What was she talking about?

"Even out of context, Jesse's the one who hurt me, and I know he didn't mean to. That doesn't make it okay, but Nameless didn't put the gun in his hand. Nameless didn't tell him to go shoot somebody. He encouraged us to stand up for ourselves, like so many of us were unable to do in the face of social isolation and intimidation."

Will turned away. Was he crying? We needed to have a talk after this. Something was up, and I wasn't in on it.

"I'm not dead," Heather reminded everyone. "I am alive. I am here, and I'm not taking this anymore."

The rest of the crowd joined us in what we all knew was coming next. "I am Nameless!" we proclaimed. Finally, we were all united in something. I wished it hadn't taken someone getting shot and the security guards declaring martial law to get there, but it happened.

I felt a buzz in my pocket and knew what that meant. Only one person who had my number wasn't already here. I read the message, grinned bigger than probably anyone expected, and pulled Mark aside as well. Cupping my hand over his ear, I let him in on it. Mark had done as much for Nameless as anyone. He deserved to know.

He followed me behind the stage, and I found his little studio setup. This was going to happen. My brave Nameless was going to do the right thing, despite the consequences he knew were coming.

LIZ

I COULDN'T BELIEVE IT. SHE WAS ALIVE! SHE WAS HERE, standing right in front of all of us.

I didn't dare step forward, especially with Veronica there, but once they went away, I nervously pondered whether or not I should make my move. Should I be offended that she didn't tell me? Should I worry about any of that right now? Did any of it matter if we could be together again?

Principal Sawyer tried to reach for Heather's megaphone yet again, and I brushed her hands away, standing between her and Heather. Heather tossed it to the floor beside the stage and let it shatter. What a badass.

She turned to me, and our eyes connected like they had in the car that night. I was overcome with emotions, but thankfully her arms were around me before I could respond, and our lips met like we'd been separated by oceans. My girl, she was here!

Static interrupted our kiss. The time had come, and I would once again share it with my love. We separated

a bit, but our hands remained clasped in pure joy.
Finally, our leader was here.

BRIAN

HE WAS PLAYING *INTO THE MYSTIC.* HE NEVER PLAYED music, let alone my favorite song. Fuck, I couldn't cry in front of all these people.

The agents started circling around, and police sirens shrieked. They were going to find him. This was the last time we would all be together like this, I just knew it.

"I promised I'd never let you down," he reminded us, "though I fear this'll be the last time we get to talk together. I have a feeling I don't have much time, so I'll make this as quick as possible."

LIONEL

THE AGENT IN THE PASSENGER SEAT FRANTICALLY banged on his car radio. "He's not using the Internet," he informed us. "He's not using the Internet at all!"

"Then how the hell is he on the air?" I asked.

"I think he's actually . . ." The agent tuned the radio to AM. ". . . on the air. Literally."

LUCAS

DRIVING IN THE CAR, ENJOYING MY LAST FEW MOMENTS of freedom, I held the mic to my face and let Mark do whatever magic he was doing. I didn't need to understand it. The roads were deserted, and I knew where everyone in town was. The reverb was reaching me, so they were tuned in loud and clear.

"They're going to find me," I admitted. "But there was no way I was going to leave you high and dry. Not now, not tonight.

"My voice may go away," I continued. "They may do all they can to suppress it, but you all have the power now. With or without me, you can keep protesting. You can keep rising up. The more all of you stand together, the less they're able to control you."

VERONICA

I WAS SO PROUD OF HIM. HE'D FINALLY REALIZED HOW important all of this was to all these kids who stood with him. To me. To us.

Peeking out around the corner, I saw every student who was there drinking in his words. The looks on their faces also read that they knew this would be it for him, for it, for all of us. "What happened at our school was horrible," he reminded us, "and it should never happen again. What caused it is just as horrible . . ."

Dammit, how was everyone in on this but me?

"But the answer is not taking away our rights," he continued while I briskly walked back around the stage to find Will. I couldn't wait anymore; some explanation was necessary.

"The answer is not throwing out anyone who has a dissenting opinion. It's much more important to know which opinions to question, and when the proper time is to speak up about them. Proclaiming your homophobia to the beautiful lesbian couple on stage? No, shove that opinion up your ass. Standing up for

270

them when Deputy Fuckface tries to profess his phony judgment on them? That's when you speak up. That's when your dissent is necessary. The marginalized need your action, not your reminders of how special you are too."

I spun Will around, and his face was red and tear-stained. "I'm sorry, Veronica," he whispered in my ear. "I'm so sorry."

"What? Sorry about what?"

"What I did to Jessica," he explained.

"What you did . . . Jessica . . ."

The pieces were forming, but I couldn't quite articulate what they were.

"Jesse," he followed up.

"You did something to Jesse?" I replied, even more confused. "What?"

"I'm sorry, Veronica," he cried. "I never meant to hurt him."

"Hurt him how?"

"I thought she was hot before," he tearfully explained, "but when he became Jesse, I thought I had the right to . . ."

"You didn't . . ."

"I did," he confirmed.

"So that's what all this is about?" I asked.

"Maybe," he responded. "Possibly. No real way to know. But Jesse didn't start wearing all black until after that night. It's my fault. Please make sure James doesn't take the fall with me."

"Take the fall?"

"I'm sorry, Veronica."

MARK

I HEARD THE CAR STOP BEHIND ME. HE WAS HERE. I HAD the microphone ready to go. For we all knew, it wouldn't be long.

He came around the corner and . . .

Lucas? It was Lucas?

Veronica grabbed him and kissed him intensely before I could inquire as to how this had all been happening under my nose and I hadn't picked up on it. No time. Questions were for later.

I handed Lucas the microphone and backed away, admittedly in awe. I'd had my suspicions, but confirming them in person was something new altogether. Lucas was Nameless.

"Now you can hear me," he spoke without anonymity, and for the first time in front of any of us, I assumed. "Unaltered, right here, right now. What Jesse did to Heather could've ended her life, but we can't pretend things like this happen right the fuck out of nowhere."

JAMES

HE KNEW, AND I KNEW THAT VOICE. I'D HEARD IT GROWL at me before, and I'd never mistake it anywhere. He'd stood up for Jesse, who we were still bullying after the incident, and I'd hit him. I'd hit Nameless. Goddammit.

I looked at Will, and he responded with a knowing glance. The façade had shattered. After all of this, we had to come clean about what had happened. For Heather. For Nameless. For all of us.

The crowd around us was understandably morose, but for a far different reason than we were. It wasn't about us right now, though.

"What we've proven here . . ." Nameless began as he reached the stage. I didn't need to turn. It was Lucas. That voice had haunted my nightmares since the day it might've caused Jesse to snap. ". . . beyond the fact that sometimes, sick fucks will take advantage of a tragedy, is that we all have something in common."

Lucas was on stage right behind us now, and I couldn't look him in the eye, knowing my role in everything that had transpired. I was ashamed. I was at fault. But I needed to hear how this would end.

"We all want to be treated fairly," he continued, "like we deserve. We all deserve love, respect, kindness, tolerance, understanding, and support . . ."

And I'd failed in that. I'd failed him. I never would again.

LUCAS

"YOU MAY HAVE STARTED BECAUSE OF LISTENING TO ME, but you all stayed here because you stood up for each other when things were unfair. You stood up for people you may have bullied, or worse. Or you stood up for those you once considered enemies, because you knew it was the right thing to do.

"Now that you have the capability of doing that, don't let it take a fucking tragedy to make it happen again. If someone's gay, let them be gay. If someone wants to be a girl, don't call them a guy, and vice versa. If someone doesn't like football, don't throw them in the garbage can. If someone's really into school, let them be. They'll probably employ you someday.

"Treat everyone like this, like this community has become. Whether or not we all believe in a god or gods or spirits or energy, we all breathe the same air and drink the same water. We are a community, not because of what separates us, but because of what brings us together. Let's remember that. Maybe that will stop the next Jesse from going over the edge."

Two cars skidded near the stage, and the countdown had begun. I turned to let the crowd see who I was instead of only facing the ones who already knew, and was greeted by a chorus of gasps. I jumped into the throng to try to buy a few more seconds. They swallowed me like quicksand, and I knew they'd hold at least a bit of resistance.

"This doesn't end here!" I yelled as quickly as possible. "Even if it does for me! Stand up, speak out, and don't take shit from anyone!"

I saw two cops working their way in from the sides, and I shifted direction. It was like running through the Red Sea out here. Cops were on the other side too. The stage was the only safe place left to go.

Other students were getting in the way of federal agents for me. For me. None of them deserved this. None of them should've ever had to put themselves in danger for me. I needed to get as much as I possibly could out . . . not for me, but for them. They needed it now more than ever.

"Say what you want," I said into the mic while dancing around, trying to blend in. "Say it loudly, and don't hold back. Say things people don't like, and stand up for the marginalized and bullied! Piss off the administration at will; they bully the gay and trans kids worse than anyone!"

I darted under the stage so I could see Mark and Veronica one more time before I was caught. "Tell people who deserve it to fuck off, and don't let them stop you from using that word, either!"

The agents saw me, and I kissed Veronica quickly before I jumped back on stage. Everything was closing in on me. This was it.

"Keep this alive! We are all Nameless!" I screamed before they finally tackled me.

The cuffs slipped around my wrist, and everyone remained there, standing . . . watching. They brought me to my feet with my arms behind me. I stared out into the sea of tears and hope, knowing that I could've avoided this, but I couldn't have lived with myself if I'd let them down. It was over.

Veronica tried to walk with me as they escorted me toward the cars. The space from the police cars were my last steps of freedom, likely for a while.

VERONICA

WHAT THE FUCK?!

DON

THERE HE WAS, FINALLY CUFFED LIKE HE SHOULD'VE been all along. Lucas, the commissioner's son. Of course!

Time to pay for what you've done to me and my school, you little bastard.

The cold steel nearly froze my hand in the night air, but I only needed one shot.

Right in front of me, his expression turned to terror.

Not so tough without your smokescreen, are ya?

"You!" I called out. "You son of a bitch, you cost me everything!"

I reached for the trigger and heard a bang.

Everything stopped. The moment was deadly silent, and Lucas and I locked eyes.

Finally. Here. Now.

Fuck, my stomach hurt. I looked down, rubbing it as I felt something poking it. Raising my hand to my face, I still couldn't see anything. How was this possible?

"What the . . . ?" I sputtered. "Crystal clear?"

Blood seeped through my shirt, and everything faded to black.

LIONEL

SMOKE BURNED MY NOSTRILS AS DON DROPPED TO HIS knees. That guy was a lunatic, and despite everything I'd learned in the last few seconds, he was still going after my son.

I dropped the gun, lamenting that after all this years, I'd finally had to use it, and the agents swarmed my son as he glanced at me. I was helpless. This was in their hands now. What a beautiful girlfriend he had too. Would they be able to make it last?

"Wait, just one second," Veronica begged.

They looked at me, as if I had any authority anymore. I nodded. What else could I do?

"Take a second," one of the agents permitted.

Veronica turned toward my son, terrified of what had just happened and yet proud of him all the same. "I love you," she told him. "I won't let them forget your name."

A smile crossed his face, despite everything, and I awaited his response. He kissed her on the forehead, unable to move his hands.

"Tell them I am Nameless," he replied as they started moving him away. He disappeared into the very car in which I'd been sitting, and the crowd began to disperse. It was over. It was all over.

What kind of day had it been? Would things ever be the same? Could they?

MISS HUNTER

"Miss Hunter," I said, reading the letter hidden with my box of belongings. "I don't know if you know who I really am, or if you're just pretending that you do, but either way, I know you're protecting your job, and all of us. You're one of the good ones, and I wouldn't want to do anything to compromise your position."

I remembered how his eyes connected with Veronica's before the agents sped away. As the crowd left the stage area, their chant modified slightly. "We are Nameless!"

They were. All of them were. And here I held the letter he'd written before that night.

"I don't know what's going to happen to me, and I don't know if I'll ever see you again, but you deserve to know everything, and I know I haven't been alone in the fight. You've been brave to stand up for what is right, even though it could've cost you your job, and I had to thank you for that."

The car disappeared into the night. Hopefully his father got him out before too long.

VERONICA

THE SCHOOL DOORS OPENED IN FRONT OF ME, AND there were no more security check points. No more long lines. No more Dons. Nameless' letter, read out loud, played through my iPod earbuds.

"We're still so young, and even if this experience ruins my record, I know that we can't just stand by and allow those in power to take everything away from us while pretending to protect us." I only hoped this assignment got to Miss Hunter before she had to leave.

No one patted me down. No one bothered me. We wouldn't have had that without him.

"Scary things happen," he continued, as if he were beside me, "and we may never be able to explain them. But we can't turn all of our schools into police states while trying to do so. At the most vulnerable times in our lives, the last thing we need to be is categorized as criminals, because we're not."

I passed by several students. I didn't recognize them, but they clearly knew me. I smiled despite this, and several hands tapped my shoulders, as if Lucas himself was letting me know that it was going to be okay.

JESSE

THE OFFICER OPENED THE DOOR, AND THEY LET ME OUT in the sun for the first time in what seemed like years. "Behavioral Health Center," the sign read.

Was this . . . What were they . . . ?

"Come on," one of them instructed. "They're waiting for you."

JAMES

THE FIVE OF US FOLLOWED VERONICA INTO SCHOOL after giving her plenty of time to have her own moment. We stepped through—the Suspended Six, as they'd called us—and the students around us began to applaud.

I blushed, knowing I didn't deserve to be recognized, and tried to hide my face from everyone. Let Liz and Heather take the stage; they deserved it.

BRIAN

"I'VE SEEN STUDENTS COME TOGETHER WHO WERE bullying each other before," Nameless reminded anyone who heard this recording, the one playing in my ear. "I've seen kids who would've never been friends form bonds stronger than any I've ever known."

I glanced at Heather and Liz as the latter helped Heather adjust her bandages. Those two—who would've thought they'd be here associating with me, or each other, for that matter? But they were perfect as perfect could be . . . here . . . together.

"I can't take credit for that," Nameless continued, "but I wish it hadn't taken such a tragedy for them to realize their empathetic potential."

LIZ

HEATHER CLUTCHED MY HAND JUST A LITTLE HARDER. The wound would never go away, but the least I could do was help her manage it. I loved her so fucking much.

"Things are not perfect," Nameless reminded us in our earbuds, one in each ear as we stayed close, "but at least they'll be better than they were when this is all said and done. I may not be there to see it, but I know you'll look after them."

Heather and I caught each other looking at the same time, and even still, after everything, we blushed a bit.

Goddammit, Nameless . . . you brought us together.

MISS HUNTER

WAITING IN THE ADMINISTRATION BUILDING, I WAS trying to finish reading the letter before my appointment. "I hope that no matter what happens, you'll still be there, trying to break through the monotony, the zero-tolerance policies, and being forced to teach the same, mundane bullshit we've had to learn every single year."

Tell me about it, kid. If I had to assign Call of the Wild again, I think I'd quit teaching for good.

The door opened, and I slipped the letter in my pocket to finish later. After all, it was the last high school assignment anyone had turned into me, and Lucas was the only one who did it.

"Miss Hunter," the navy-suited lady asked.

"Yes?" I replied.

"We heard about your work in the city. We're pleased to have you on board."

"Thank you so much," I responded with as much gratitude as I could muster.

LIONEL

THE AGENTS LED LUCAS TOWARD ME. MY SON. EVEN with the trouble he was in, I was nothing short of proud of him. The quiet kid who stayed in his room all the time had been doing what he felt was right. How could I not admire that?

His gaze connected with mine, and I put a hand on his shoulder. "Dad?" he whispered.

"We're going home, son," I said.

"But . . . how?"

"Someone owed me a favor." The mayor wasn't thrilled about it, but after I'd stopped Don, she couldn't exactly say no.

I walked toward the car with my son. Probation, community service, and reinstatement all lay ahead, but this time, I'd let him tell me what he needed instead of the other way around. I hoped this, if nothing else, let him know that he could talk to me as himself, and not need to be anonymous with me or Martha.

"I'm sorry, Dad," Lucas said.

"No," I corrected him, "do not apologize to me."

"But I . . ." he stammered.

"I won't hear of it, or I'll let them take you back," I replied with a smirk. My son was coming home. No way I'd let any of those charges stand. He'd stood up for his entire school at his own personal risk. He couldn't be implicated in the wrongdoing.

Jesse was headed to a behavioral health center to get the care he really needed, now that he was no longer facing a potential murder charge. Miss Hunter had been hired by one of the prestigious schools in the northeast. And Veronica would surely come see him after he got home.

What a peach! My son sure had good taste, just like his old man.

VERONICA

MISS HUNTER'S OLD ROOM, WHERE HEATHER WAS SHOT. They'd cleaned everything up and repurposed it, as we knew they would. Four years from now, nobody with living memories of what had happened here would be around. No one would have firsthand memories of the one who'd united us all.

"For you," he spoke in my ear, "for all of us, I'm sorry I never told you."

I wondered if he'd recorded this for everyone, or just me. Either way, I had the last episode of Nameless' podcast in my ears, and Lionel had mentioned he had a surprise for me when I got off school. Life was getting back to normal . . .

Or as normal as it could ever be again for us. We were forever changed, and that was for the best.

"I am Nameless," he said at last, concluding the letter. Someone watched *Perks* before writing it. His Logan Lerman impression was uncanny.

Turning back toward the hallway, where once chaos had roamed, normalcy had returned. Up there, near the place where he'd been beaten up, I swear that for a second, I saw him. I saw Lucas, as his dad had informed me after laughing about his son's coy nature. He smiled and winked at me, and I returned it, even though I probably looked crazy waving at someone who could no longer be there.

Tonight, I'd go on. I had something to say and a story to tell. First episode of my own podcast, or at least the continuation of what he'd started.

"I am Nameless," I repeated out loud, to myself, and it was true. Now it was my turn. Later, anyway. After the surprise.

I closed the door behind me, and awaited what new lessons we'd learn in English with our third teacher of the year. It didn't matter though; no one would ever match Miss Hunter.

We were Nameless. We were infinite. And we were together. I'd have my Lucas back somehow, somewhere, some way, and this time, I'd be a voice that he could be proud of. He was Nameless, The Voice in the dark when we all needed one, and the love of my life.

"I am Nameless," I silently reminded myself as I took a seat and began a new chapter, both in the book and in all our lives. The darkness was gone, finally, and now there was only hope in the dawning of our senior year.

Heather's eyes met mine for a second, and we shared a smile, knowing what we'd all gone through to get there. She placed some of the flowers to the side of her desk, gently touching Liz's hand next to her as she leaned, and the two gave everyone a bad case of the warm and fuzzies with how sweet they were together.

Soon, I'd be together again with my Nameless. My Voice. My Nameless. My Lucas. And my name, all of our names, all together—taken back. For good.

ADDITIONAL ESSAYS

TO SPEAK UP

Melina Rayna Barratt

To speak. To speak up! To be. To be in front. To be visible. To be seen. To be heard. To speak up *and* be heard.

Sometimes, it's to challenge. Sometimes, it's to give comfort. Sometimes, it's to learn or to educate. Sometimes, it's to participate or to be included. Most often, for me, it's all of this.

I challenge bad ideas, which left alone would continue to hurt people. I bring comfort to those who are being hurt by those bad ideas, let the victims know there is someone trying to make it stop. Someone cares, someone sees them and their struggle. I seek to teach others why those ideas are bad and how it hurts people. We are people too, we belong, we are part of society, and we deserve to have our voices heard.

Why? Why "rock the boat"? I "pass," so why not just fit in? Why do I have to make a spectacle of myself? Why do I call attention to myself and the fact that I am trans? Why do I bother?

When I spoke to the Marion County School Board last year, a bunch of local students approached me. They thanked me profusely for my words though I wasn't the only one to speak in support of them. One even cried in my arms. I know people that are afraid of going outside or using the bus. I know people who have been fired for being trans. I also know someone who has been made a VP of Diversity in a major national bank in part *because* she's trans.

At many of the forums and events I have attended or participated in, I am regularly approached by strangers thanking me for being out and open. They know someone—usually a family member—who is trans, and they appreciate the problems many of us experience. They say I am brave, some say courageous.

But am I?

I don't fear going outside, I am a student not yet ready to go back into the workforce. I have insurance, doctors who know what they are doing, a family that is mostly supportive and financially able to do so when needed. I live next to a county that is very progressive and I feel safe enough in my home county. I have never been afraid of police, and have connections with a number of elected officials. What am I really risking when I go out, when I wear a "trans and proud" t-shirt in public? Many live in daily fear, but I don't. Does that make me brave?

When I think of courage, I think of that boy who, surrounded by many who were actively trying erase him, was able to tell me his truth. I think of the courage it takes him to simply live through the day, go to school and be reminded of how much the people around him might hurt him every . . . damn . . . day.

Why do I speak up? Because I would feel like a coward if I didn't.

LUCKILY

Noah Lugeons

Luckily for my twelve-year-old self, he didn't want to play any of those stupid reindeer games anyway. He had more important stuff to do. He was actually hanging out alone in his room again because he *wanted* to.

I mean, he hadn't been invited to the thing (he'd actually *never* been invited to the thing), but even if he *had* been invited, he'd have said no. After all, his bedroom wasn't exactly gonna hang out in itself, was it?

He continued to tell himself that as he moved from the bed to the beanbag chair, and popped *Bionic Commando* into his Nintendo. He'd only beaten that game in a single sitting two dozen times, after all.

That was probably why he'd chosen to hang out by himself again, he realized. Because he knew that the twenty-fifth time one beat *Bionic Commando* was universally held to be the most satisfying. And so, after a liberal oral aeration of the Nintendo, he set off to defeat Hitler's resurrected corpse once more.

At this point, his thumbs were on autopilot, and his mind was able to drift to the thing again. He supposed the people at the thing were having fun. Not "beating *Bionic Commando* for the twenty-fifth time" levels of fun, obviously; but fun nonetheless.

And if he'd been one of those "at the thing" types of people, he supposed he'd probably be having fun, too. He wasn't, obviously, but he *could* have been, so he supposed there was no harm in considering what it might be like to be one of those people who got invited to the thing.

And the more he thought about it, the better it seemed. So much so that eventually he had to stop thinking about it.

Of course, there was no mystery as to why he never got invited to the thing. It took him a little longer than most to figure out the bounds of social acceptability, but he *had* figured them out. He just routinely ignored them. If he wanted to get invited to the thing, all he'd have to do is listen to that little voice in his head that said, "You probably shouldn't say that" a little more often.

But to hell with that voice; it was wrong.

That voice was more worried about getting invited to the thing than it was about being right, so to hell with that voice.

I mean . . . yeah, okay, maybe he *shouldn't* have said it. But it was right, wasn't it? David *was* being a bully. Stacey *was* being mean. There *was* no hell. That poem *was* awful. Those were all objectively true statements, so why should he regret having said any of them?

Well . . . he didn't. He didn't regret it at all. Because

if it wasn't for that, he would probably be at the stupid thing tonight, instead of bionically grappling his way through the Third Reich.

Luckily for my nineteen-year-old self, he didn't really care about accuracy or truth, because otherwise, he wouldn't have been able to stand being at the thing.

And the thing, by the way, was *amazing*. The thing was filled with cheap alcohol, expensive weed, beautiful women, and robust laughter. It was the absolute *picture* of a good time.

So who cared if the whole purpose of the thing was to pretend we could summon protective spirits from the Akashic dimension to reverse global warming? I mean, sure, it was bullshit. It was profound bullshit. But none of that mattered, because damn it, he'd finally been invited to the thing.

What's more, people at the thing really liked him. He knew a lot of random facts about every type of bullshit. He read palms and cast hexagrams and interpreted tarot, and as long as he pretended like it wasn't utter nonsense, they kept letting him come to the thing. Heck, they were even happy to see him when he got there.

And sure, sometimes he had to actively censor himself. When that girl who insisted everybody call her "Raven's Breath" started telling them about the psychic conversation she had with her corgi, he'd had to work pretty hard not to laugh.

And when one of the six long haired dudes with goatees and tie-dyes clearly just told somebody their aunt should ignore her doctor and trust in the power of herbs and positive thinking, it seemed downright immoral not to say anything.

And when Heather showed up at his apartment later, as gullible as she was gorgeous, and asked if he was serious about helping her develop her telepathic abilities, there was no real way to justify his response, so he didn't even bother to try.

Well, he supposed that wasn't entirely true. He had *tried* to justify it, but he'd failed. No matter what complicated cerebral yoga he employed, he couldn't morally justify what he was doing. He wasn't just ignoring lies—he was actively promoting them.

And it wasn't like they were harmless. He'd seen genuinely ill people eschew medicine because of them. He'd seen people ignore sound life advice in favor of what the I Ching told them. He'd seen people fleeced by gurus who offered absolutely nothing for the low, low price of whatever they could afford.

And he'd been an active part of every aspect of that. Justifying his role in it would have been a task far more herculean than ignoring it, so he opted for the latter.

And it wasn't like he didn't have any help in so doing. Whatever he thought of himself, other people sure seemed to like him a lot more now. When he was true to himself, and said what he really thought, people excluded and ostracized him. When he parroted bullshit and never let ethical considerations get in the way of a fun lie, people included and admired him. If he figured the math democratically, it didn't matter that he didn't much care for himself. He was outvoted. And all the other people who were voting had the exclusive right to invite him to the thing, so their votes were the only ones that really counted.

Luckily for my thirty-six-year-old self, he'd had a lot of practice not saying anything, because this time was gonna be like the final exam of holding his tongue. The girl couldn't have been more than ten years old, and her crime was reading a book.

And it wasn't like it was *Mein Kampf*, or the novelization of *Two Girls, One Cup*, or anything. The entirety of the crime was that it was a book, and she was a girl. And books weren't for girls, according to her Hasidic father.

And as he watched this man berate a child for her curiosity, and explain in thickly accented English that this knowledge was only for boys, he started to shake and hoped it wasn't visible. He felt like surely he should say *something*, but that had only ever caused trouble before. He'd have to be flattering himself to pretend he could string together a couple sentences that were going to talk this asshole out of his religion.

But he could at least say *something*. He could turn to the dad and say, "You should be ashamed of yourself." He could turn to the daughter and say, "There's never anything wrong with learning." At least he could let her know that somewhere in the world, there were people who disagreed with her father and valued her brain without regard to the genitals it was indirectly attached to.

But by the time the train slowed to a stop at the Forest Hills station, he'd resolved to ignore it. He was good at that, after all. Hell, just that week he'd ignored somebody at work recommending his chiropractor to another coworker, his roommate lauding the wonders of his homeopathic immune-system booster, a guy in the locker room quoting Plato and attributing it to the Bible, sixteen people of various breeds of zealotry pushing pamphlets at him on the streets, his boss telling him about this great productivity webinar he signed up for, his friends spouting misogynistic remarks about every attractive set of legs in Central Park, his employees wailing about the dangers of genetically modified foods, and an entire city government around him vocally defending a "search all the brown people" policy.

He'd been practicing the art of holding his tongue for decades, and worst case scenario, it would cost him a sleepless night. In his experience, saying what he really thought almost always cost more than that.

So when the train doors slid open, he walked passed that sexist father and that helpless daughter wordlessly, but it a lot harder than he thought it would be. And it kept him up for a hell of a lot longer than a night.

And as he lay awake replaying that moment, and the echoing decades of silence that led up to it, he started to realize that silence, despite its golden reputation, was pyrite.

After all, he'd already been to the thing, and to be honest, it wasn't all it was cracked up to be. He had toed the tightrope between censored and censured for decades, and as he lie awake over the next few nights, he came to fully understand the illusory value of popularity bought at the price of honesty.

And though he'd known where it was this whole

time, he found his voice again—and the next time he found himself in a situation like that, he said something.

For the last five years, I've been paying a penance for my silence. When I was young and desperate for acceptance, I allowed my peers to beat the voice out of me. And even though I knew where it was the whole time, it took me decades to find it again.

Silence, as I learned, was the most addictive drug of all. Because silence is acceptance, and acceptance breeds acceptance. My willingness to ignore my morals, my education, and my rational mind were met with nothing but social reward. My efforts to correct the record, no matter how egregious the crime, were met with nothing but isolation.

But in the end, I came to realize that every time that voice in my head said, "You should really say something," it was right. And when I finally forced myself to confront the real costs of my silence, I couldn't help but be ashamed. So now I spend my days exploring the voice I spent my life trying to subdue, all in hopes that I can help usher a few others to the same conclusion.

The inherent wisdom of age is often overplayed, and at forty-one, I'm not exactly sporting a wizard's beard worth of life experience, but there are a few things that forty years of memories teach you. And one that should have been more obvious to my younger self is that way more of your life is spent in the long run than the short.

And in the long run, you never regret doing the right thing.

IT'S DANGEROUS TO GO ALONE

Matthew O'Neil

Mental health has sort of been "my thing" for as long as I can remember.

I remember seeing a doctor when I was about ten who, after stories from my parents of my poor behavior, attitude in school, and my struggle to connect with other kids my age, suggested I see a psychologist.

"We don't want you setting fires to people's houses," he joked. I didn't find the humor in it.

My family struggled though, and I was never brought to see any mental health specialists. Instead, my family urged me to try different approaches to my problems. Being that no one—at least no adult—in my family had any mental health experience or expertise, none of it really helped.

As I grew older, I would hide as the panic attacks set in, I would isolate myself to listen to music and, eventually, to learn to play guitar. Once I reached college, I discovered what I believed to be the medical benefits of self-medicating with alcohol.

I saw counselors while in school, attempting to help me break the cycle of substance abuse, but it was all for nothing. I almost dropped out of school, even with one semester left the urge to leave was overwhelming but they somehow talked me out of it. I hated the people around me. I hated the school. I hated myself. It never reached a point of seriously considering self-harm, but it would be a lie to say those types of thoughts never entered my head.

A decade after graduating, I had eventually stopped drinking. It took a failed marriage, several attempts at serious careers that never took off, and offending my second wife while black-out drunk to make me turn it around, but that didn't take care of the problem. It took care of the symptom. Ending the substance abuse didn't end my mental health woes.

Time without alcohol was agonizing. Lacking a social lubricant, I approached each and every social encounter with a racing heart, tense muscles, sweat pouring down my back.

My second wife, who insisted I needed to "get over" the anxiety I experienced, had a tendency to make remarks that made socializing worse for me. She told people she feared having children with me because of my ex-partner's physical appearance, worrying that any children we might have would take on those characteristics (your guess is as good as mine as to why this was relevant or even made sense).

She openly told people about mistakes I made while drinking, that the men in my family had a thing for blondes, and she even belittled a friend of mine who was present, referring to him as "Band-Aid" because he had been hit by a car while crossing the street and sustained some serious injuries.

I couldn't stand being around other people with her in the room. I didn't want to be around other people after she spoke to them. I resented her, and I hated that she didn't understand that it was embarrassing when she told intimate details about my mental health. I wasn't a husband; I was a punchline.

One morning, in December of 2016, I woke up knowing I was suffering from low blood sugar. I've been diabetic since I was seven, and the first thing I was taught was if you know your blood sugar is low, you get something to eat.

As I ate I started to feel normal again, but something felt off. My wife attempted to hold a conversation with me, but I struggled to communicate. In my head, I could clearly think through everything I wanted to say. Yet when it came to actually articulating my thoughts, I couldn't say more than a word or two before my mouth stopped working. I tried writing out my thoughts, but even that was a futile effort. It came out as garbled on paper as it did from my own mouth.

One E.R. trip later, we were able to see that I had not, in fact, had a stroke like I feared. Instead, my low blood sugar had been so low that it triggered a panic attack. Even after my blood sugar was back to a normal level, I couldn't talk or write out thoughts. The hospital gave me liquid Ativan, and almost immediately I could talk again. As much as I had wished to stay on Ativan, as I had originally been prescribed by my doctor, they refused to give me a regular prescription for it because of my history of substance abuse.

There were numerous problems that exacerbated my mental health issues, including the inevitable dissolution of my second marriage, but one other instance stood out and truly redefined my view of my own mental health and the relevant issues around it.

In April of 2017, I was in my office. I worked, at the time, in a state prison offering rehabilitation services to sex offenders. Next door to me was a case worker's office, and she would regularly see the inmates we worked with for various issues. On this particular day, she welcomed an inmate in who had a history of assaulting staff. And he assaulted her.

I called for help, but the officer on duty, who was a new hire fresh out of the corrections academy, froze. Someone on the other side of the unit heard my shouts and called for assistance. I could not intervene as I had no training in self-defense or any safety training for dealing with physical confrontation, so I stood by helplessly as the case worker was beaten.

Eventually, staff arrived and stopped the inmate. He was taken away in handcuffs and later charged with the assault.

And I turned into an anxious mess.

In spite of the best efforts of the staff on hand, and those later asked to come in and speak with us, it was pointed out that I was exhibiting symptoms of PTSD. My boss, a clinical social worker, thought my low blood sugar episode might have triggered it. My therapist was sure that, if I didn't have it before, then the assault most definitely caused it. And I suddenly found myself falling down another bottomless pit of mental health disorders with no clue how to handle myself.

Sleep became a rare thing. And if I ever did sleep, and had dreams, they were recurring events of the assault. I started questioning my own worth in the world, assuming that my mental health struggles were more of a burden on others. That my children would be better off with no father rather than one that started crying because he left their hotdogs on the stove a minute longer than they should've been.

It was when these feelings started hurting me the most, particularly around the issues of self-harm, that I started talking to people about it. The first person I told was my sister, and then my parents. While it wasn't ideal, they were the people whom I'd put through the ringer the most with my mental health issues and would understand the best, especially if I was taking ownership of my condition.

I talked with my boss and counselor about techniques and coping skills to prevent me from having meltdowns at work, outbursts when I was alone, even methods to help me sleep. I opened up to my girlfriend, whom I told a lot to already, and it acted as a sort of therapy to unburden my heart and head with the chaotic thoughts. Being that she studied psychology, it was also amazing to have a support that was nonjudgmental and supportive. And the medication my doctor prescribed. Let's not downplay that factor.

Eventually, what I had discovered was something I had been advocating the inmates I taught: Your social support system was your best resource. People knowing these details about you can be options and opportunities to help you cope with stress and symptoms of your condition.

More importantly, you never know who's going through the same struggles as yourself. While I haven't acquired a network of others struggling with PTSD or similar anxiety disorders, I have found some that know my struggle. That empathize with me. I've even helped others see that this isn't a condition relevant only to war veterans.

My boss had always stated, "Don't go out on the branch alone," or, "Don't go upstairs by yourself." Like with any other struggle, doing it by yourself is the worst way to manage. Similar to the concept of "it takes a village to raise a child," no one should struggle with life's challenges, be they health, financial, family, etc., alone. As advocating for myself and opening up to others has helped me, in what little time has passed since developing my mental health disorders, the same can be seen in others who find success with their own troubles.

Don't be left out on the branch alone. Speak up, speak out, and speak often.

THE POWER OF A MOMENT

Karen Garst

In the spring of 2017, an eight-year-old boy hanged himself with a necktie after having been bullied and knocked unconscious at school. Explaining his injuries away, the boy said he had just fallen and of course, no one who saw the incident reported it. Neither did the boy tell his mother. Instead, he took the final action of suicide. This is an extreme example of bullying where no one challenges the perpetrator, and even if seen, no one told the principal.

Unfortunately, these incidents are not isolated. It is less likely that incidents similar to this story happened when we lived in small tribes. Everyone knew each other, and an adult was almost always present to intervene when things got out of hand. But as we started to live in larger groups and form larger and larger villages, and then cities, the morals that were passed down by the tribal leaders became harder to instill in everyone.

Thus, tribal relationships transformed into moral laws. Because religion was the same as the state, these laws were often codified in religious writings. Many religions have a version of the Judeo-Christian admonition called the Golden Rule: "Do to others what you want them to do to you."[1]

The earliest version, recorded around 2000 BCE, is attributed to the Egyptian goddess Ma'at and states, "Now this is the command: Do to the doer to make him do."[2] Confucius stated it as follows in 500 BCE: "Never impose on others what you would not choose for yourself."[3]

Many other early civilizations adopted some form of this adage. People had lost their connections to the others they lived around, not seeing them as "I" or "self." It is usually the case that someone bullies someone who is seen as different. While there are still hunter gatherer tribes, most of us live in a neighborhood, village, city, or country where we frequently interact with people we do not know.

But having a rule that is promulgated to educate people in proper behavior is clearly not enough. The person who beat the young boy in the first paragraph obviously didn't follow it. What is needed, as illustrated in Marissa's story, is someone to speak out. First performed by the anonymous "Voice," then taken up by the mass of students, eventually someone speaks up about the bullying. What does it take to speak up?

First, it is necessary to learn empathy. As stated above, if you see those who are different from you as "the others," it will be harder to speak up for them. Empathy can be achieved and learned in several ways.

Look in the mirror. Imagine that you were the one that was hit or bullied. Can you see yourself in that position? Can you imagine what it would have felt like?

The second step might be to talk to the victim afterward. "I am so sorry that happened, are you okay?" This might start a dialogue with the victim where you learn how it felt to him or her. Young people might start with those that are made to sit alone in the high school cafeteria. Sitting down and talking to someone who is treated differently than you is a true learning experience. It is easier to do this than to intervene, but that will come later.

Second, everyone needs a parent or mentor to get them started, to teach them what is right and wrong and to call them when they forget. I clearly remember an incident in fifth grade where a friend and I were teasing a new girl that had arrived at our school. I don't remember what we said to her, but she told her mother, and her mother called my mother and I got a talking to. She explained why that would hurt someone and tried to get me to empathize with her.

Because of this intervention and our apologies to the girl, we soon became best friends. But not everyone has a parent who knows how to do this. Imagine a child who has been abused his/her entire life by a parent. They are never going to learn the lessons of how to treat others.

Third, give up on the expectation that there will always be someone else to do it instead of you. That is simply not going to happen. There will be people who grow up to be adults who have never had the courage or nerve to intervene in a dangerous situation. We always hear about the hero who comes to the rescue, but we need more heroes, and you can learn to be one.

Fourth, learn to be confident enough to be able to speak out. This is a long road. I was so shy in high school that I never would have spoken out. But gradually, I learned. I recall an incident in graduate school where I was a teaching assistant. The TAs had a union and we had gone on strike against the university. I had been president of the organization earlier and was now one of the spokespersons for the union.

However, I was so surprised to attend a meeting of the women TAs who wanted to pick someone to "speak for them." I clearly remember standing up and saying, "I don't think the guys are doing this. We each need to speak up for ourselves and make our views known." To think this occurred in a group of highly educated women shows just how timid people are about standing up in a crowd and expressing a viewpoint, to say nothing about intervening in a situation where there is a bully or a threat is being made against someone.

Fifth, once you are able to speak up, you have to train yourself to intervene at the appropriate moment. When Will kicked the young boy was the optimum time. But think of all the pressures that those in the small crowd felt. *What would Will think of me? Would Will hit me if I said something? Could I tell the principal in confidence without revealing who said it?* That is asking a lot of a young person.

The other problem in this story is that the school police officer is a jerk. Who would want to tell him anything? This was not the case during my childhood. We had a police officer from the city (they weren't in schools yet full-time) come and visit us throughout the year. Everyone loved him! He was a short man we all called Mack. I remember feeling safer because of him and he taught us without scolding or chiding. We learned a lot from him. But who would want to tell the school cop in this story?

The other factor in the story is the restrictive atmosphere where even commenting about a book gets you in trouble. Nothing feels safe anymore.

Finally, you have to reward yourself when you do speak out. Get a special dessert, go to a movie, talk to your parents, tell a friend. It's okay to learn to feel good about speaking out. It makes you more likely to do it again. And once you have done something that you were previously afraid to do, you will find yourself saying, "Hey, I did that. I can do that again."

We are never going back to the days of my youth where everyone grew up in a small town. Everyone knew everyone else. We interacted not just at school, but at church, at sports events, and other celebrations in the city throughout the year. No, we are moving to cities like Los Angeles or New York, where you might know people in your school, but rarely see them outside of class. And the classes and schools are so large, even having a large group of friends is difficult.

That is why the message of Marissa's story is so important. We all must learn to speak up when we see or experience bullying behavior.

[1] Matthew 7:12 NCV
[2] https://en.wikipedia.org/wiki/Golden_Rule
[3] Ibid

COMING OUT OF THE MENTAL HEALTH CLOSET

Dr. Gleb Tsipursky

My hand jerked back as if the computer mouse had turned into a real mouse. Would they think I was crazy? Would they whisper behind my back? Would they never trust me again? These anxious thoughts ran through my head as I was about to make a post revealing my mental illness to my Facebook friends.

Whenever the thought of telling others about my mental illness entered my mind, I felt a wave of anxiety pass through me. My head began to pound, my heart sped up, and my breathing became fast and shallow, almost like I was suffocating. If I didn't catch it in time, the anxiety could lead to a full-blown panic attack, or sudden and extreme fatigue, with my body collapsing in place. Not a pretty picture.

For six months, I had been suffering from a mood disorder characterized by high anxiety, sudden and extreme fatigue, and panic attacks. I really wanted to share much earlier. It would have felt great to be genuinely authentic with people in my life and not hide who I was. Plus, I would have been proud to contribute to overcoming the stigma against mental illness in our society, especially since this stigma impacts me on such a personal level.

Ironically, the very stigma against mental illness, combined with my own excessive anxiety response, made it very hard for me to share. I was really anxious about whether friends and acquaintances would turn away from me. I was also very concerned about the impact on my professional career of sharing publicly, due to the stigma in academia against mental illness, including at my workplace, Ohio State University, as my colleague and fellow professor described in his article.

Still, I did eventually start discussing my mental illness with some very close friends who I was very confident would support me. And one conversation really challenged my mental map, in other words how I perceive reality, about sharing my story of mental illness.

My friend told me something that really struck me, namely his perspective about how great it would be if all people who needed professional help with their mental health actually went to get such help. One of the main obstacles, as research shows, is the stigma against mental health. We discussed how one of the best ways to deal with such stigma is for well-functioning people with mental illness to come out of the closet about their condition.

Well, I am one of these well-functioning people. I have a great job and do it well, have wonderful relationships, and participate in all sorts of civic activities. The vast majority of people who know me don't realize I suffer from a mental illness.

That conversation motivated me to think seriously through the roadblocks thrown up by the emotional part of my brain. Previously, I never sat down for a few minutes and forced myself to think what good things might happen if I pushed past all the anxiety and stress of telling people in my life about my mental illness.

I realized that my mind was just flinching away, scared of the short-term pain of experiencing anxiety and stress of sharing about my condition. This flinching away prevented me from really thinking clearly about the long-term benefits to me and to others of sharing my story of making the kind of difference I wanted to make in the world and being authentic with people in my life. I recognized that I might be falling for a thinking error that scientists call hyperbolic discounting, a reluctance to make short-term sacrifices for much higher long-term rewards.

To combat this problem, I imagined what world I wanted to live in a year from now—one where I shared about this situation now on my Facebook profile, or one where I did not. This approach is based on research showing that future-oriented thinking is very helpful for dealing with thinking errors associated with focusing on the present.

In the world where I would share right now about my condition, I would in the short term be anxious about what people think of me after they find out.

Anytime I saw someone who found out for the first time, I would be afraid about the impact on that person's opinion of me. I would be watching her or his behavior closely for signs of distancing from me. And this would not only be my anxiety: I was quite confident that some people would not want to associate with me due to my mental illness. However, over time, this close watching and anxious thinking would diminish. All the people who knew me previously would find out. All new people who met me would learn about my condition, since I would not keep it a secret. I would make the kind of difference I wanted to make in the world by fighting mental stigma in our society. Just as important, it would be a huge burden off my back to not hide myself and be authentic with people in my life. This would be a great benefit to me in the long term.

I imagined a second world. I would continue to hide my mental health condition from everyone but a few close friends. I would not be making the kind of impact on our society that I knew I would be able to make. I would always have to keep this secret under wraps, and worry about people finding out about it. I would always be stressed about hiding my true self, always worried about people somehow finding out, always and feeling like a hypocrite. Always regretting the chance to make the kind of impact I knew I could make. Moreover, likely people would find out about it anyway, whether if I chose to share about it or some other way, and I would get all the negative consequences later.

I shuddered when I imagined that kind of life. With

that shudder, I knew that the first world was much more attractive to me. So I decided to take the plunge, and made a plan to share about the situation publicly. As part of doing so, I made that Facebook post. I had such a good reaction from my Facebook friends that I decided to make the post publicly available on my Facebook to all, not only my friends. Moreover, I decided to become an activist in talking about my mental condition publicly, as in this essay that you are reading. I also published articles about my condition in prominent academic media channels (*Inside Higher Ed* and *Diverse: Issues in Higher Education*) to challenge the stigma against mental illness in academia. I also shared my story with a local newspaper, to raise awareness of mental health and deal with stigma against mental illness.

What can you do?
So how can you apply this story to your life? Whether you want to come out of the closet to people in your life about some unpleasant news, or more broadly overcome the short-term emotional pain of taking an action that would help you achieve your long-term goals, here are some strategies.

1. Consider the world where you want to live a year from now. What would the world look like if you take the action? What would it look like if you did not take the action?

2. Evaluate all the important costs and benefits of each world. What world looks the most attractive a year from now?

3. Decide on the actions needed to get to that world, make a plan, and take the plunge. Be flexible about revising your plan based on new information such as reactions from others, as I did regarding sharing about my own condition.

What do you think?

- Do you ever experience a reluctance to tell others about something important to you because of your concern about their response? How have you dealt with this problem yourself?

- Is there any area of your life where an orientation to the short term undermines much higher long-term rewards? Do you have any effective strategies for addressing this challenge?

- Do you think the strategy of imagining the world you want to live in a year from now can be helpful in any area of your life? If so, where and how?

66962664R00187

Made in the USA
Lexington, KY
29 August 2017